"The ponies!" Alice cried. "My father—he's going to kill them!"

Dave looked at her, horrified. "Kill them? How could anyone kill the ponies?" Dreadful pictures began to fill his mind—Flash and Bluey, after years of service, dragged up from the mine shaft, to be cast off and replaced by machinery. It couldn't happen!

Then, slowly, an idea began to form—it was a daring, dangerous scheme, but worth it to save the pit ponies!

The Littlest Horse Thieves

by

Rosemary Anne Sisson

Based on the
Walt Disney Productions' motion picture

Screenplay by
ROSEMARY ANNE SISSON
Story by
BURT KENNEDY and
ROSEMARY ANNE SISSON

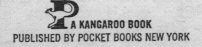
A KANGAROO BOOK
PUBLISHED BY POCKET BOOKS NEW YORK

THE LITTLEST HORSE THIEVES

POCKET BOOK edition published April, 1977
2nd printing.........................July, 1977

This original POCKET BOOK edition is printed from brand-new
plates made from newly set, clear, easy-to-read type.
POCKET BOOK editions are published by
POCKET BOOKS,
a Simon & Schuster Division of
GULF & WESTERN CORPORATION
1230 Avenue of the Americas,
New York, N.Y. 10020.
Trademarks registered in the United States
and other countries.

ISBN: 0-671-80960-1.

Printed in the U.S.A.

To Charles Jarrott,
who made it all come true.

AUTHOR'S NOTE

IT is the novelist's proud boast that he did it all himself. But with a film, a hundred talents come together to give substance to, and breathe life into, the original script. If I were to thank all those whose art has found its way into these pages, I would need to name every single member of the film unit. So all I can do is to thank Hugh Attwooll and everyone, in Burbank, Pinewood and Yorkshire, who gave their hearts to making the film, *Escape from the Dark* [American title: *The Littlest Horse Thieves*], and most particularly to the marvelous cast and to Charles Jarrott, upon whose emotional and imaginative vision I have shamelessly but gratefully drawn.

But more directly I must also declare my indebtedness to Burt Kennedy for the story idea, to Ron Miller and Frank Paris who set me off on the right track at the start, and to the Walt Disney Productions librarians for invaluable research, to Lord Robens for encouragement and assistance, to Gerald Thompson, Tom Dobbin, Kenneth Kay and Isaac Gurney who showed me and explained to me for the first time the world underground in Dudley Colliery, to the late Tom Hall of Carhouse Stables, and to Bill Charlton whose long experience as a Mine Manager shrewdly guided us before and during filming. Above all, my most grateful thanks are due to Peter Heap, who read the film script and the novel at every stage, and saved me from a hundred foolish errors. I confided to him at the very beginning my ambition that we should be able to show the film to an audience entirely composed of miners, and not once have them shout out, "rubbish!" If the same could be true of this novel, it will be mainly due to the generosity of Peter Heap.

R.A.S.

The
Littlest
Horse
Thieves

CHAPTER ONE

THE mining village of Emsdale lay unobtrusively in a fold of the Yorkshire moors—unobtrusively but for the winding wheels which stood on big black legs above the colliery.

To the outsider, the pit-head would have looked like a ramshackle collection of wooden sheds and red brick buildings, set in a sea of black dust and sludge. But to Dave and Tommy it all had a meaning and a purpose just as familiar as the big black kettle in their mother's kitchen or the mangle in her wash-house. The only neat and tidy part of the colliery was the Manager's office, which was set above the yard, with the other administrative offices. They had green-painted doors and were reached by an iron staircase. Dave had never been up there. Much more important to him was the red brick building, beneath the winding wheel and beside the engine-house, which housed the pit-shaft. This was the heart of the colliery, where miners plummeted down some 600 feet into the earth to dig the coal which was at once their livelihood and their enemy.

When Dave took his disc from the tally-man and stepped into the cage, he felt that he was going into a world where no one could reach him. It was true that Luke was a miner, but he worked at the coal-face. He didn't usually bother Dave and Tommy in the stables.

At the thought of Luke, Dave felt the familiar tightening round his jaw and mouth and he scowled, and his young brother, Tommy, glancing up at that moment, looked surprised, but then scowled, too, because he always did what Dave did. Dave gave Tommy a shove to relieve his feelings, and Tommy looked surprised again, but then Dave

11

grinned at him, and he grinned back, showing a great gap
where his two front teeth were missing.

The cage dropped into the darkness. Wind roared by,
and water dripped down the brick tunnel which seemed to
rush upwards past them. There were maintenance workers
in the cage with them, the safety lamps they held glimmer-
ing in the dark, but they didn't speak more than a word or
two. No one ever spoke much as they dropped down into
the dense blackness of the pit.

The gate of the cage clanged open and shut, and the men
stepped out, and walked away along the wet, black level to
the small desk where the Deputy was waiting to set them
to work. Dave and Tommy turned aside and hurried along
the short passage which led into the stables.

"Hey up, lads!" cried Bert, the old Horsekeeper. "You're
early. You've even raced old Flash for once."

Bert had a face like a nut-cracker, and no teeth. "How
do you eat your dinner, Bert?" Tommy had asked him
once, and Bert had grinned his toothless grin and said,
"Munch, munch, munch, like a horse eats hay!"

Bert had begun to work in the pit when he was a boy of
twelve, sitting all day by the ventilation doors and pulling
a string to open them as the ponies hauled the tubs of coal
to and fro. Then he became a driver, working with his own
pony, and running behind him from the coal-face where
the miners dug the coal to the "landing" where it was unloaded to be brought up to the surface. Now, too old for
such hard work, he was in charge of the stables, looking
after all the ponies which worked in the pit.

The stables were small, with whitewashed arches, and
looked much brighter and more airy than the rest of the
coal-mine. Each stall had the pony's name painted in white
on a brown board, and some of the ponies were already in
their stalls, their coats matted with sweat and coal-dust,
waiting to be groomed and fed. On the concrete slab outside, Bert was busy washing Bluey, a little blue skewbald
with a wicked eye. Tommy went to help him. Bluey was a
particular favorite of Tommy's, even if he did have a
nasty habit of kicking out at you when you least expected
it. Perhaps it was because Tommy, going through life in
his happy-go-lucky, seven-year-old ways, always *was* getting clouted when he least expected it, so Bluey made him
feel at home.

Dave was always uneasy until Flash was safely back in

the stables after his shift. Ponies could be involved in accidents down the mine, just as men could, and Flash was working right up at the forward heading, with Luke and his partner, Amos. Dave hated to think of Flash hauling the coal for Luke. Wasn't it enough for Luke that he had married Dave's mother? Did he have to have the best pit pony as well?

There was a rattle of harness, and a clip-clop of little hooves, and Flash came nipping round the corner and trotted briskly into his stall, shaking his bushy, particolored top-knot.

"Eh, Flash, you found your way, then?" said Bert.

"Flash can find his way anywhere," said Dave, proudly.

"Anywhere in the pit, that's true," said Bert, taking hold of Bluey's halter to lead him back to his stall.

"So can Bluey," cried Tommy, loyally, moving quickly to avoid a left-jab from Bluey's wicked little off-hind hoof.

"Nay," said Bert with a chuckle, "he's a good 'un is Bluey, but he's only a young 'un. He's not as knowing as Flash is, but he'll learn."

Flash's driver had unhitched the heavy iron frame called the limber-gear which hooked on to the tubs, and had left Flash to make his own way from the landing to the stables, so he was only wearing his leather harness and the bridle with the protective iron eye-pieces. Dave began to unfasten the buckles, while Flash nuzzled him for the crust of bread and jam which Dave always managed to sneak out of the larder when his mother wasn't looking. It was a bit fluffy from the inside of Dave's pocket, but Flash was used to that. When he was unharnessed, cleaned and groomed, showing his thick brown-and-white coat, Dave reckoned that, despite his cropped tail and short, bushy mane, Flash looked as fine as any pony in Yorkshire.

"I wish we could take the ponies up above ground, Bert," he said. "They do in some pits, don't they? Once a year, for a holiday. And they have competitions for 'Best Pit Pony' and all. I've seen pictures in t'paper."

He suddenly saw himself proudly leading Flash out in front of the judges as they declared him the winner, and then riding him through the main street of Emsdale, carrying the silver cup on which were inscribed the words "FLASH, EMSDALE COLLIERY, BEST PIT PONY, AUGUST 1909."

"Nay," said Bert, "they're better down here, doing the work they know."

A rough voice spoke from the entrance to the stables.

"Dave! Tommy!"

Dave, just coming out of Flash's stall, turned his head. He knew who it was, but he had discovered that it made Luke angry when he just stared at him without speaking, so he did it as often as he could.

"Don't be too long," said Luke. "Your mother will have your tea ready for you."

Dave looked back at him in silence. Even under the coal-grime, he saw Luke's face harden, and the blue eyes narrowed angrily as Luke frowned. Tommy, coming out of Bluey's stall, glanced from Luke to Dave, aware that something was going on, but not quite sure what it was.

Luke turned on his heel, his great boots clattering on the stone floor, and Dave smiled, and then Luke turned back, and Dave felt a breathless instant of alarm, because he knew that Luke had seen the smile. But Luke pretended that he hadn't and called out to Bert, who was just emerging from the back of the stables with a bundle of hay.

"You'd best get the boys out of sight, Bert," said Luke. "The Gaffer's coming."

He turned and went out without looking at Dave again. Dave let his breath go in relief. He hated being afraid of Luke, but he was. Luke was such a big man, and had such a hard face and a loud, rough voice. When Dave defied him, as he did all the time, he knew quite well that Luke could knock him to the floor with one blow of his great fist. He never had yet, but one day he might, if Dave went too far, and somehow knowing this made Dave go on trying to provoke him into it, even though he was afraid—or perhaps, *because* he was afraid.

"Who's 'the Gaffer'?" asked Tommy.

"New Manager," Bert answered. "Only arrived today. They say new brooms sweep clean, but he'll have his work cut out, I'm thinking, in Emsdale."

"Will the Manager sweep the stables, too, then, Bert?" inquired Tommy, fascinated.

"Nay," said Bert, with a wink at Dave, "nobody works in my stables without I say so, not even t'Manager. Now, come on, get hid behind them bales of hay, like your father says."

Dave, moving with Tommy towards the far end of the stables, stopped short, and looked back at Bert.

"He's not our father."

"Your stepfather, then."

"He's not our father," repeated Dave, obstinately.

There were footsteps in the passage, and the sound of voices.

"Come on, quick!" said Bert, and shoved Dave and Tommy out of sight in the nearest empty stall.

Crouched down behind Bert's bandy legs in their corduroy breeches, Dave didn't dare look up, but he heard, uncomfortably near, the voice of the Overman, Sam Carter, saying, "This is the Horsekeeper, sir, Bert Cawsden," and he saw Bert's arm move as he touched his cap.

Tommy, fidgeting as usual, rustled about in the straw, and Dave saw Bert stiffen, and shift round a bit to try to hide them better. Dave glared at Tommy. Supposing the Manager thought it was a pony in there, and came to have a look at it? Dave knew quite well that they weren't really supposed to be there. Boys weren't allowed to work in the pit now under fourteen years of age, and he was only twelve. Bert was glad of the help in the stables, and the old Manager, Mr. Oakroyd, never bothered about things like that. But Dave knew what a "new broom" was. It was someone who'd come new to a job and was going to show everyone what's what. Maybe if the new Manager found them there, he'd think he had to show them that he was a new broom by telling them to get out and never come down there again. And since the ponies never came up above ground . . .

Dave thought that if he should ever be parted from the ponies, there wouldn't be anything left in life which was worth bothering about.

Dave saw between Bert's legs the big, heavy boots of Sam Carter, the Overman, and beside them a pair of rather small, neat boots, shiny under all the splashes of wet coal-dust. He heard the new Manager's voice speaking in a funny, almost foreign way, with the words very clipped round the edges.

"These ponies are very small."

"They have to be for our levels," said Sam.

"Yes."

Dave knew that in some pits, the passages were high enough to allow the use of quite large ponies—almost like cart-horses—but at Emsdale there were places where the levels were no more than five feet high, and even the shortest man had to stoop a little.

The trim, shiny boots moved away, and Sam's followed. Bert threw an expressive grimace at Dave and Tommy over his shoulder, and then took a few steps forward.

"They can't haul more than two tubs at a time?" inquired the Manager.

"Nay, sir!" Dave could hear the surprise in Sam Carter's voice. "Each of them tubs weighs more than eight hundredweight."

"Hmm . . ." said the Manager. A few more steps, and then, "How long has this one been down here?"

"Fourteen year," Bert answered.

"And he would be three or four years old when he came down? He must be past his best now, then."

Dave knew very well which pony the Manager was looking at. Sheer indignation made him jump, and the straw rustled, but the Manager was some distance away now. Bert laughed.

"Old Flash?" he said. "He's the best worker of them all. And he's that clever, he hardly needs a driver."

"That's right," said Sam Carter. "Flash always knows his way to the coal-face, and back to the stables."

"And he knows when his shift's over," said Bert.

"Aye, he does that!" said Sam. "You'd've laughed this evening, Bert. You know he's got a new driver—that young lad they call Ginger? Well, at the end of the shift, Ginger thought he'd get some empty tubs up for the morning, and he tried to turn Flash round. You should have seen him kick! So Luke Armstrong, he says, 'You're wasting your time, lad,' he says. 'Old Flash knows when his shift's over, and he knows where he's going. You may as well turn him loose.' "

Sam Carter laughed aloud, and Bert chuckled, too. But Dave could just see the new Manager's face through a crack in the stall, and he wasn't laughing at all. He looked rather stern, and thoughtful. He nodded to Bert, and turned on his heel and went out without another word, and Dave caught a glimpse of Sam Carter's face as he turned to follow him.

" 'Night, Bert," he said, and Dave knew that he was trying to sound as though he was saying it for the Manager as well.

Dave stood up, and Tommy began to crawl out of the straw, and then Dave quickly dropped down again, and grabbed Tommy to keep him still. The Manager had paused with Sam Carter just outside the stables.

"Have you ever seen a main-and-tail hauler?" he said.

"I've heard of 'em," Sam replied. "I've never seen one."

"It can handle a hundred tubs at a time," said the Manager. "Brings the empty ones in, and takes the full ones out."

"Oh, aye?" said Sam.

Their footsteps clattered along the passage, and Bert turned and grinned at Dave, and nodded to show that they could come out.

"What was he talking about?" said Dave.

"Some kind of machine, I suppose," said Bert. "They get some funny ideas, do Managers."

"Fancy him saying that about Flash!"

"Aye, well," said Bert, tolerantly. "He's nobbut a London fellow. He doesn't know much. Come on, lads, you'd best be off to your tea."

CHAPTER TWO

RICHARD Sandman stood in his office, fixing the collar-stud at the back of his shirt. He had taken his overalls off, and washed his face and hands. The miners came out of the pit with their teeth shining white in their black faces, and went home to a tin bath in front of the kitchen fire, but Mr. Sandman knew that his wife would hate him to bring coal-dust into her clean, neat house, with ornaments everywhere and white lace antimacassars on the back of the chairs.

As he began to put his tie on, Mr. Sandman was staring

out of the window, but he wasn't looking at the big black
winding wheels turning above the pit-head, or at the miners
as they stepped out of the cage with their lamps and
trudged across the yard to the gates which had the words
"Emsdale Colliery" in wrought iron above them. Mr. Sandman was thinking. He had to make the colliery pay. Somehow he had to make the colliery pay.

Mr. Sandman suddenly stiffened. He had, after all, seen
something through the window—two figures much smaller
than the others which were emerging from the cage. Mr.
Sandman opened the door of his office.

"Carter!" he called.

Sam Carter turned. The light from the gas-lamp on the
corner of the Manager's office fell on his big, square face,
and he gave a quick frown.

"Who are those boys?" asked Sandman.

Sam Carter moved very slowly towards him.

"Boys, sir?" he said, innocently. And then he met Mr.
Sandman's eye, and coughed. "Oh—them boys, there. Aye.
Well. They're just—Dave and Tommy Sadler. They help
the Horsekeeper with the ponies."

"They look too young to be on the payroll."

Sam looked embarrassed.

"Well—they just . . . Bert gives them a penny now and
then. They like to do it, and he's—he's getting on a bit."

Mr. Sandman frowned.

"They've no business to be going down the pit," he said.
"Apart from anything else, there are safety regulations to
be considered."

A big man spoke unexpectedly from among a group of
miners standing near by.

"No business?" he said. "I reckon that pit belongs to
them, if it belongs to anyone. Their father died down
there."

The front door of the Armstrong house opened straight into
the kitchen from the main street which ran down the village
of Emsdale. When Dave stepped inside, with Tommy behind
him, he saw that Luke was sitting in the armchair by the fire
where once his father used to sit. Luke's face was now
white instead of black, and he had on a clean shirt. Dave
knew that his mother would have helped to bathe him in
the tin bath in front of the fire, as she had once helped to
bathe his father, scrubbing his back with the blue-black

scars on it, and fetching the towel from the brass rail in front of the stove.

Violet Armstrong came out of the scullery in her faded sprigged cotton dress and big white apron, and stopped short at the sight of Dave and Tommy. She had a round, pretty face, and fair hair which she did her best to draw back into a bun in the nape of her neck. But somehow little curls kept escaping and spoiling the effect, just as a smile usually twitched the corner of her mouth when she was trying to eye the boys severely, as she did now.

"Oh, you're back then!" she said. "If it's not too much trouble, perhaps you'd have a wash and get sat down for your tea!"

Meals were the worst time for Dave. At other times, he could keep out of his stepfather's way, but when they sat down at table, there was Luke, sitting opposite his mother, clattering his knife and fork and passing his cup up for more, just as though he had a right to be there. And Dave and Tommy had to sit on each side of him, while their mother waited on him.

"Was it a hard shift today, Luke?" asked Violet, as she put her own plate on the table, and sat down.

"No more than usual," Luke replied. Then he looked up, and met Violet's eye, and shrugged. "It's a narrow seam, and low down. And we're getting that far in . . ."

"It's dangerous," Violet finished.

"No!" said Luke, and Dave looked up quickly at the rough tone of his voice, and saw his mother fold her lips.

Luke took a bite of gammon and eggs, and spoke with his mouth full.

"It's just that it's a long way to fetch the coal back. It's hard to make a decent wage."

Violet had just picked up her knife and fork, but she paused, holding them in the air.

"They'd not close the pit, would they?"

Dave and Tommy looked up, startled. Almost everyone who lived in Emsdale worked at the pit. The houses were colliery houses which belonged to the owner of the mine. How could the pit be closed? You might as well talk about closing the village!

"Nay!" said Luke. "Not while the owner can make a penny or two out of it, they won't!"

Luke grinned, and Violet looked relieved and began to

eat, but Dave's eyes were on Luke's face, and he thought the grin didn't last long. Then Luke glanced at Dave, and Dave quickly looked away and polished his plate with the last of his bread and butter and crammed it into his mouth. He always ate as fast as he could, because that made it less time to sit at table with Luke.

"Dave!" said his mother. "That's good food you've got there. Be thankful for it, and don't just gobble it up as if it was nothing."

Tommy took another thick slice of bread and butter, and Dave glared at him, but Tommy pretended not to see.

Luke cleared his throat.

"How did you find Flash today, Dave?" he asked. "He's got a new driver, you know."

Dave shrugged and buried his face in his coronation mug. He knew that Violet would speak, as she always did, to cover up when he didn't answer his stepfather.

"How did he get on?" she asked.

"He doesn't know much about ponies," Luke answered, "but old Flash'll soon teach him."

He smiled, and Violet smiled, and then they both looked at Dave—hopefully, as though they thought he might smile, too.

Dave took a final gulp of tea, put his mug down and stood up, looking at Tommy. Regretful but obedient, Tommy swallowed his last bite almost whole and prepared to get up.

"Where do you think you're going?" said their mother.

"Going to take Pearl for a run," replied Dave.

The fawn-colored whippet heard her name from her box by the fireplace and uncurled herself.

"It's a bit late, isn't it?" said Luke.

Dave kept his eyes on Violet's face.

"We always used to take Pearl out last thing," he said.

"Yes, but not alone!" said Violet, and then stopped short, and Dave knew that she was remembering that it was their father who had always pushed his chair back and said, "Come on, lads, let's take Pearl for a run before you go to bed."

Luke suddenly banged his great fist on the table, so that the cups jumped and rattled.

"Oh, go!" he shouted violently. "Go, why don't yer?"

Tommy looked frightened and scrambled off his chair. He headed for the door and the whippet slithered out of her box and crept after him. Dave followed them to the door and pushed Tommy through. Luke's violence had frightened him, too, but he felt at the same time an uncomfortable sort of triumph. Luke might be bigger than he was, but Dave knew he had made Luke do something he didn't want to. Before he closed the door, Dave heard Luke say roughly, "I'll have some more tea!" and saw his mother's face, expressionless, as she held out her hand for his cup.

There was nearly always a chill wind off the moors, even on a summer evening like this one, but it brought a honey-sweet scent of heather with it. Dave and Tommy ran down the village street and scrambled up the path behind the colliery, with Pearl racing ahead. They scampered along the hillside, and slithered down into the hollow above the pit-head. It was their own special hiding-place, and, while Pearl ran about trying to raise a rabbit, Dave and Tommy lay on their stomachs in the springy grass and looked down into the colliery yard. There was no night shift, and the maintenance-men were all below, so the yard was almost deserted, but the light was still on in the Manager's office.

"Do you remember when we used to come here with me father?" said Dave.

"I think so," said Tommy, doubtfully.

Dave turned on him.

"You *must* remember! You *must!*"

Tommy looked puzzled.

"We've got to remember him," said Dave. "Because if we don't, it's as though we make him dead."

"He *is* dead," said Tommy, with that awful reasonableness of his.

He scrambled to his feet, and set off up the hill again.

"Come on, Pearl! Come on!"

"He isn't!" Dave shouted after him. "He isn't dead!"

Tommy paused, startled, and looked back.

"Not as long as we remember him," said Dave.

CHAPTER THREE

THE Mine Manager's house stood outside the village. As Richard Sandman walked up the lane towards it, and pushed open the small garden gate, he had a feeling of pleasure and relief. It was a neat, stone-built house with a white rambler rose growing round the porch, and a mellow light shone from the oil-lamp behind the lace curtain in the drawing-room. Mr. Sandman stood still for a moment, enjoying it all, and then he turned the brass door-handle and went inside.

Packing-cases stood about in the small, square hall, and, as Mr. Sandman took off his bowler hat and turned to hang it on the hat-stand, Alice ran out of the drawing-room, clutching a china ornament.

"Oh, Father!" she cried. "I thought you'd never get home!"

She flung her arms round his waist and hugged him, and Mr. Sandman hugged her back.

"Alice!" called Mrs. Sandman from the drawing-room, "mind you don't break that piece of china!"

Alice hastily withdrew it, and she and Mr. Sandman looked at it together. It was a statuette of a smug-looking little boy in red bloomers, with his hand resting on the neck of a feeble-minded lamb, but fortunately both he and the lamb were still intact. Alice grinned at her father, and he found himself grinning back. He knew that his wife would have preferred Alice to be a neat, well-behaved little girl, with teeth like pearls, who kept her white frilly dresses clean, and sat in a corner all day nursing a doll. But he couldn't help being glad that Alice had a wide, generous mouth, and fair curly hair which always escaped from its black bow, and that, whenever he came in, she was so glad to see him that she rushed into his arms and nearly knocked him over. He knew that he wasn't popular with the men at work. It wasn't important, he told himself, that they should like him. What mattered much more was that they should respect him, and that he should get the best work out of them. But still, it meant a lot to him to know that when he came home, Alice would run to meet him with her great brown eyes glowing with pleasure, and that she at least believed that whatever he did was right.

"Look, Father," she said, "Clara and I have unpacked all the pictures. Haven't we worked hard?"

"Very hard," he answered, and smiled at Clara, the maid, as she came into the hall to rummage about in the packing-cases for more bric-à-brac. "I see you've hung all the curtains, too."

"Clara did that," said Alice. "I only held the step-ladder."

"Well done, Clara," said Mr. Sandman, and Clara's rosy face, roughened by the Yorkshire wind, broke into a wide beam.

The Sandmans had brought their cook, Mrs. Green, from London with them, but the little Cockney maid-of-all-work had flatly refused to come, saying that nothing would make *her* go up to that nasty North, why she didn't even like visiting her auntie in Enfield. So Clara was a miner's daughter from Emsdale who'd been in service as a kitchenmaid at the Rectory, and was very proud of her promotion to house-parlormaid.

"Mother's putting the best china away," said Alice. "She wouldn't let me help with it. She said I might drop it."

She grinned again, and Mr. Sandman shook his head at her, but he was smiling as they went together into the drawing-room.

"Hullo, dear," said Mrs. Sandman, turning away from the corner cupboard. "You're back."

She said that every evening, and it used to annoy Mr. Sandman, but he didn't mind it now. It was part of coming home.

"Had a good day, dear?" he asked, going to kiss his wife. As a matter of fact, he said that every evening, too.

"Not too bad," replied Mrs. Sandman, taking the ornament from Alice. "But I shall be glad when I've got the house in order. I hate to see it so untidy."

Her husband laughed.

"Considering the fact that we only moved in yesterday, it looks very tidy indeed. My dear, I think you have done wonders."

"Oh, do you really?" said Mrs. Sandman, pleased. "Now, where shall I put this ornament?"

"Um——" Mr. Sandman felt that he should show some interest. "How about on the mantelpiece?"

"Ye-es," said Mrs. Sandman, thoughtfully. "Now, which end?"

"I really don't think it matters," said Mr. Sandman.

He sat down with the copy of *The Times* which he hadn't had time to read at breakfast, and Alice sat on the arm of his chair, while Mrs. Sandman tried the ornament first on one end of the mantelpiece and then on the other. She had a bundle of soft brown hair and very round blue-gray eyes, and Mr. Sandman was always fascinated by the way she could give her entire attention to such things as the exact length of a curtain, or whether or not to wear a brooch at the neck of her lace blouse.

"Cook says, do you want your supper now, Mum?" inquired Clara from the doorway.

Mrs. Sandman stiffened.

"Thank you, Clara," she said, her voice suddenly very genteel indeed. "Now that the Master is home, you may serve *dinner*."

"All right, Mum," said Clara, cheerfully, and vanished.

Mrs. Sandman closed her eyes for a moment.

"That girl!" she exclaimed. "I do wish she would call me 'Madam.' 'Mum' is so vulgar!"

A moment later, an enthusiastic hammering on the gong made Mrs. Sandman close her eyes again, and summoned them to the dining-room.

"How did you find things at the mine, dear?" asked Mrs. Sandman, when Clara had put the soup in front of them, and Mr. Sandman had said grace.

"Not very good," Mr. Sandman answered.

Alice plunged her spoon into Mrs. Green's oxtail soup, but her eyes were fixed intelligently on her father's face.

"I hope you won't have to do anything too unpopular," said Mrs. Sandman, nervously.

Mr. Sandman's voice hardened.

"I've been brought here by Lord Harrogate to make his colliery pay," he said, "and I'm going to do it. If I don't, he'll close the pit down, and then I shall lose my job, as well as the miners' livelihood."

"What exactly is the problem, dear?" inquired Mrs. Sandman. "Alice! Do try to drink your soup more quietly!"

"Sorry, Mother," said Alice. She always meant to remember, but there seemed to be so many more important things in the world than drinking soup quietly.

Mr. Sandman took a piece of bread and began to crumble it up into small pieces and drop it in his soup, but Alice knew that he wasn't thinking about that, but about the colliery.

"The real problem," he said, "is that we can't get the coal out in sufficient quantities, and therefore it is too expensive. At that price, we can't sell it. We can't even sell the coal we *do* get out. That's why they had to stop the night shift."

Mrs. Sandman's attention had already wandered to the sound of Clara dropping a dish-cover in the kitchen, but Alice was listening intently.

"What will you have to do, Father?" she asked.

"Well, for a start," said Mr. Sandman, "I shall try to get rid of those pit ponies."

CHAPTER FOUR

WHEN the whistle blew in the morning, it was as if the whole village of Emsdale was tilted up by a giant hand, and all the men who lived there were swept down into the pit. One minute there was no sign of life except for the smoke rising from all the chimneys as the wives cooked breakfast. Then the colliery whistle would blow, and suddenly the street was full of men in black clothes and heavy boots, swinging their lamps and tramping along like a ragged army. One by one the doors would open, and the miners would emerge, greeting their mates and falling into step beside them, trudging on towards the big black winding wheels etched against the pale sky, and turning beneath them through the wrought-iron gates into the grimy colliery yard.

Dave and Tommy, taking a short cut through the yard next morning, with Pearl at their heels, saw Luke standing waiting outside the cage with his mate, Amos, and four or five other miners.

"Dave!" called Luke.

Dave turned, hostility in his face. Luke walked towards them.

"You might take Pearl up to the traps if you like," he said, "give her a bit of training. I'm going to race her next weekend."

Dave shrugged and ground a piece of coal into the dirt with the toe of his boot.

"We might do, or we might not," he said.

He turned and went towards the fence, stooping between the bars. Tommy began to follow him, but Luke called sharply after him.

"Tommy!"

Tommy looked up at him, apprehensive.

"Come here," said Luke.

Tommy dawdled towards him, his left bootlace dangling. Dave paused on the other side of the fence, and looked back, frowning. He saw Luke stoop down and wind the bootlace round the battered little boot, and tie it firmly in a double-bow. Luke straightened up and put his hand gently on Tommy's shoulder.

"Go on," he said. "Off you go."

Dave saw Tommy give Luke a little smile, and then remember that he wasn't supposed to, and he ran quickly towards Dave. Dave turned and scrambled up the hillside. He felt angry and uncomfortable, though he didn't know why.

It was several hours later when Alice opened the back door and scampered through the back garden towards the small gate which opened straight on to the moors. She wore a sailor-suit, a shiny black straw hat, black stockings and buttoned boots, and she was carrying a paper kite, its tail streaming behind her. Mrs. Sandman opened the casement window of the dining-room and leaned out.

"Alice!" she called. "Where are you going?"

Alice knew better than to stop.

"Just going to fly my kite, Mother," she shouted over her shoulder, and opened the gate and ran through, leaving it to bang behind her.

Mr. Sandman, coming round the corner of the house, saw his wife leaning out of the window, and turned to watch the small, flying figure.

"Don't go too far!" Mrs. Sandman called. She looked at her husband and sighed. "I don't like her going out on the moors alone."

"It'll be a bit lonely for her here at first. I expect she misses all her friends in London."

"Still," said Mrs. Sandman anxiously, "I don't want her playing with any of those rough miners' children."

"Oh, she has too much sense for that!" Mr. Sandman replied.

"I shall be glad when the governess arrives," said Mrs. Sandman, "to keep her out of mischief."

She closed the window, and Mr. Sandman's lips twitched as he looked after Alice, who, by now, was scrambling on all fours up the steep path in a thoroughly unladylike manner. He found himself wishing that he could go and help Alice to fly her kite, instead of keeping his appointment up at the Big House with Lord Harrogate.

The odd job man brought the horse and trap round from the stable, and, as Mr. Sandman climbed up into the seat and took the reins, Mrs. Sandman came out to see him go. He hoped that his wife did not know how very nervous he felt. He had never met the owner. The letter offering him the post of Manager of Emsdale Colliery had come from Lord Harrogate's agent, and all the arrangements had been made through him. But on arriving at his office, he had found a note in very black writing on very thick white paper which simply said, "Come and see me on Wednesday at 10 A.M. Harrogate."

"I hope His Lordship is agreeable, dear," said Mrs. Sandman.

"So do I," said Sandman.

The horse's hooves seemed to make a great deal of noise as Mr. Sandman drove along the private road which led through the park. There were deer grazing among the huge oak and chestnut trees, and swans drifted on the lake which Capability Brown had created out of a sluggish brook a hundred years before. As he came in sight of Harrogate House, Mr. Sandman reined back the horse, and sat for a moment, looking at it. It was an Elizabethan stone house, with a wide terrace looking out over the lake, and a carved doorway above the big oak door. Mr. Sandman squared his shoulders, gathered the reins more firmly and drove on.

A supercilious butler opened the door. He didn't speak, but merely raised his eyebrows, glancing towards the groom who had come to the horse's head as though he wondered whether Mr. Sandman should not have driven round to the back entrance, instead of boldly up to the front door. Mr. Sandman was wondering the same thing himself, but decided to put a brave face on it.

"Mr. Sandman," he said firmly, "to see Lord Harrogate."

"Oh yes, sir," replied the butler, without enthusiasm. "His Lordship is expecting you."

He stood aside to allow Mr. Sandman to enter, and took his hat from him. Mr. Sandman wished that he had followed his wife's suggestion and bought a new bowler hat "for best." His old one looked very shabby on the highly polished table inside the door, and the black ink which Mrs. Sandman had used to conceal the bald spots just looked shiny.

"His Lordship is in the conservatory," said the butler.

He led the way across the big hall in a stately manner. Mr. Sandman wondered how he managed to walk so quietly. His own boots made a terrible clatter on the black-and-white marble floor. The butler opened a glass door at the end of the hall.

"Mr. Sandman, m'Lord," he said in a tone which seemed to indicate that, if his master had hoped for great things from his visitor, he was likely to be disappointed.

Lord Harrogate was a tall man. He wore a tweed Norfolk jacket and knickerbockers, with heavy knitted woolen socks. His feet were remarkably long, and were encased in brown boots with pointed toes. A halo of fluffy white hair rose above a high forehead and he had very bright blue eyes which at the moment were fixed intently upon a pot of orchids held in his hands.

"Come in, Sandiman," he said, "come in. What do you think of my orchids?"

"Well—er . . ."

The last thing Sandman had expected was to be asked to give an opinion on orchids. Lord Harrogate looked brightly up at him.

"Splendid, aren't they?"

"Er—splendid, my Lord," said Sandman, feeling that it was expected of him.

He glanced round the conservatory. It was extremely hot, and he could already feel the sweat beginning to pour down his face. An extraordinary arrangement of pipes curled itself round the glass erection, and an ominous hiss of steam emerged at intervals from a valve near the door.

"You see," said Lord Harrogate, happily, "I have a piece of machinery here—it's called a thermostat—that keeps the conservatory at the same temperature all the year round. Result—perfect blooms!"

He glanced at the dial of the thermostat, and in that instant, Sandman noticed with dismay that the perfect bloom in Lord Harrogate's hand had quietly dropped to the floor. Lord Harrogate looked back. Where the perfect bloom had been, nothing remained but a bare green stalk.

"Oh," said Lord Harrogate. "How very odd."

He tapped the valve, which hissed at him in a menacing manner, and Lord Harrogate backed away, put the pot down on the shelf and firmly trod on the orchid bloom, pretending that it wasn't there.

"Now," he said, "what did you want to see me about?"

But before Mr. Sandman could reply, Lord Harrogate observed that the butler was still waiting in the doorway.

"Yes, Barker," he said. "What is it?"

"Excuse me, m'Lord," said the butler, austerely, "but you asked to be informed when the electric machine was used in the kitchen for the first time."

Lord Harrogate's face brightened instantly. The defection of the perfect bloom was forgotten.

"Splendid!" he cried. "Splendid! I'll come at once."

He set off for the door. Feeling slightly dazed, Mr. Sandman stood aside, but Lord Harrogate waved an inviting hand towards him.

"Come on, Sandiman," he cried. "This will interest you."

In the huge kitchen, housemaids, footmen and kitchenmaids stood around, looking with some apprehension at an elaborate electrically turned spit which was suspended over an old-fashioned coal-fueled stove. The cook, a round-faced, stout woman, with gray hair under a large white cap, had just skewered a pheasant on the spit, and stood back, eyeing it with extreme distrust and dislike as Lord Harrogate charged into the kitchen, followed by Mr. Sandman.

"Good morning, Mrs. Ramsbottom," cried Lord Harrogate. "Ah, good. I'm glad you're using that at last. Splendid. You see, Sanderton, it's an electric spit."

"Oh, yes, my Lord," said Sandman.

"Great improvement," said Lord Harrogate. "It used to have to be turned by the bootboy. Much better now, eh, Albert?"

A rather fat boy stood in the doorway which led to the scullery.

"Yes, m'Lord," said Albert, in reply to a glance from one of the footmen, but he didn't say it with any great enthusiasm. It occurred to Mr. Sandman that Albert probably enjoyed the rather peaceful task of turning the spit, and also got a lick or two of fat into the bargain.

"This is the machine of the future," exclaimed Lord Harrogate, happily. "Ready, Mrs. Ramsbottom?"

"Yes, m'Lord," said the cook, with dire foreboding.

"Then I'll just turn it on," said Lord Harrogate.

Full of happy anticipation, he pulled down the switch.

"There now," he said. "The spit will turn of its own accord."

Mr. Sandman found himself watching as breathlessly as everyone else. The spit, with a loud humming noise, made several lurching turns and then, with a sort of casual deliberation it dipped down and allowed the bird to sag into the fire.

"Oh, my Lord!" cried Mrs. Ramsbottom.

Lord Harrogate looked dismayed for a moment, but soon recovered.

"Ah, not quite right yet," he said. "I'll just—ouch!"

In attempting to replace the bird more firmly on the spit, he had burned his fingers.

"Here, you, boy!" he said. "Come and put the bird on again."

"Yes, m'Lord," said Albert, with some reluctance.

"Oh, don't bother, m'Lord," said Mrs. Ramsbottom. "I'll use the old spit, and Albert can turn it."

"No, no," said Lord Harrogate, licking his burned fingers. "We'll soon have this working for you. There you are. Now, Sanderton, switch it on."

Sandman dutifully pulled down the switch again. The spit turned round twice in a stately manner.

"There!" said Lord Harrogate. "Excellent!"

Mrs. Ramsbottom looked pleasantly surprised. The spit turned again, made an even louder humming noise, and then neatly and with determination precipitated the pheasant into the fire. Mrs. Ramsbottom stared at it in speechless indignation, and then looked at Lord Harrogate.

"Ah," he said. "Still not quite right. Never mind, Mrs. Ramsbottom. I'll get the electrician up from London. Probably some quite small thing wrong with it."

"Yes, m'Lord," said Mrs. Ramsbottom, grimly.

She eyed the bird, sizzling quietly in the fire.

"Don't worry," said Lord Harrogate. "We'll get it working for you."

"Thank you, m'Lord," said Mrs. Ramsbottom.

Lord Harrogate turned and briskly departed, followed by Mr. Sandman. Before he left the kitchen, however, Mr. Sandman had time to see that Albert had made the mistake of grinning from ear to ear, and as a result had received a tremendous box on the side of the head from the aggravated Mrs. Ramsbottom.

Mr. Sandman was still feeling some amusement as he followed Harrogate along the kitchen passage, through the green baize door and across the hall, so it was something of a shock when, as they entered the library, Lord Harrogate suddenly turned, looking directly at him with those bright blue eyes, and said, "Now, then, Sanderson, what about my colliery?"

"Oh—well . . ." said Mr. Sandman, stammering slightly, ". . . er—one of the problems, my Lord, is that Emsdale is a small colliery, and the coal-faces are a long way from pit bottom, so that . . ."

"Yes, yes, yes," Lord Harrogate interrupted. "I daresay."

He walked forward into the dark, book-lined room, with its tall windows looking out over the park. Mr. Sandman hesitated, and then took a few steps after him. He didn't want to remain standing just inside the door, like a servant. On the other hand . . . Lord Harrogate turned towards him again.

"When are you going to stop it making a loss?" he inquired.

"It doesn't make a loss, my Lord, exactly."

"It doesn't make a profit either," Lord Harrogate grumbled. "Kirkdale's Colliery makes a profit. Why can't mine?"

"It is a question of fetching out enough coal to be able to sell it at a reasonable price."

He saw from Lord Harrogate's face that he had not won his unstinting attention.

"I should like to explore the possibility of using machinery in the pit," he faltered.

Lord Harrogate's face instantly lit up.

"Machinery!" he exclaimed. "Sit down, my dear fellow, sit down."

"Thank you, my Lord."

Mr. Sandman perched on the edge of the leather sofa, and Lord Harrogate sat in an armchair opposite, eyeing him expectantly, like a dog which confidently expects the bestowal of a large bone.

"You mean," he said, "that we can use machines in the pit instead of miners?"

Mr. Sandman took a breath, and then let it go again. Could Lord Harrogate be serious? He wasn't sure. He took another breath.

"Er—no, my Lord," he said. "But it might be possible to bring the coal from the face to the shaft by means of machinery instead of ponies."

"Really?" cried Lord Harrogate, delighted. "Splendid! Splendid!"

Glad to have engaged Lord Harrogate's interest at last, Mr. Sandman prepared to explain further, but he found that the owner's eyes had wandered past him.

"Those damned rabbits are on the lawn again!" he exclaimed.

He leaped to his feet and darted to the window, peering out. Mr. Sandman stood up, not sure whether to continue or not.

"Er . . ." he said.

Lord Harrogate glanced at him, surprised.

"I was wondering, my Lord . . ."

"Yes? Yes?" said Lord Harrogate, but half his mind was clearly on the trespassing rabbits.

"I should like to explore various possibilities," said Mr. Sandman, "but in the first instance, I should like to consider installing electricity, so that we can draw on the most up-to-date equipment."

"Electricity, eh?" said Lord Harrogate. "Yes. Yes, by all means. Look into it, and let me see some plans."

He flung the window up, seized the shot-gun which stood in the corner and let fly at the rabbits with both barrels.

CHAPTER FIVE

"ARE we going up to the traps?" asked Tommy, as he caught up with Dave on the hill above the pit-head.

"No!" said Dave quickly, and then he added, "We're not going there just because *he* said so."

Tommy wiggled his nose.

"Pearl could do with a bit of training," he said.

Dave didn't answer.

"We always used to take Pearl out training," said Tommy. "Then if she won, me father used to give us a penny."

"I daresay," said Dave, "but," jerking his head back towards the pit, "we don't want *his* pennies."

As far as Tommy was concerned, a penny was a penny, but he knew better than to say so. He walked along in silence for a bit, and then remarked, "But I like it when Pearl wins."

Dave paused, and hesitated. So did he.

"All right," he said. "Come on."

And he raced away along the path which led up to the traps, with Tommy and Pearl scampering after him.

It was glorious up on the moors. White clouds went scudding along across a blue sky, and the heather, in full bloom, had turned all the slopes and hollows as far as the eye could see to a rich, glowing purple.

The whippet traps consisted of wooden crates, with a door in front which could be raised by pulling on a piece of string.

"There's many a race been won in the traps," Dave remembered his father saying. "By Goy, there may be dogs as is faster than Pearl, but she comes out of that trap like a bullet from a gun."

Then Luke had laughed (because Luke and Dave's father used to be mates, and worked together up at the coal-face) and he said, "*I'll* get meself a dog one of these days—and I'll get Dave and Tommy to train him, and then we'll see who wins!" And he had ruffled Dave's hair, and then they had all laughed.

But it wasn't Luke's dog that they were training now, it was their father's, and they were training it for Luke.

Dave pulled the string, and Pearl shot out, and bounded away towards Tommy, who was yelling to her and scuttling away as fast as he could, until she overtook him and he fell over his feet and rolled in the heather and Pearl climbed all over him, licking his face.

"Let's do it again!" cried Tommy, happily dragging Pearl back towards the trap.

"No," said Dave. "Don't want to tire her."

"She's not tired," said Tommy.

"Well, I say she is!" said Dave, and cuffed him.

Tommy's face crumpled up, and he drew his lip into the space where his front teeth used to be.

"Oh, don't be such a cry-baby!" said Dave, walking away.

"I'm not crying!" said Tommy, but David heard a sniff behind him, and he walked faster because he knew he ought to say he was sorry, that he didn't mean to do it. He knew it wasn't Tommy's fault that his father wasn't there any more, and that Luke was, but whenever he felt he couldn't bear it for another moment, Tommy always seemed to be the only one around whom he could clout, and so he clouted him.

When he heard the cry, Dave thought at first that it was Tommy calling after him, and he paused and looked back. But Tommy was stumbling along with his lips pressed together, sniffing.

"Did you hear something?" said Dave.

Tommy shook his head, and sniffed again. Then they both heard it together.

"Help! Help!"

Pearl heard it, too, and went racing away over the brow of the hill, barking furiously. Dave and Tommy ran after her, and looked down into the hollow.

"It's a girl," said Dave. "Up a tree!"

Pearl, a whippet of limited intelligence, appeared to be under the impression that she had treed a rabbit. She was still barking, with her forefeet up the trunk, but when Dave slithered down the slope, she stood courteously aside, as though inviting him to have a go instead.

Dave looked up the tree. He saw a little girl in a grubby sailor-suit, with her hat hanging down her back by its elastic, and fair hair tumbled about her flushed face. Alice, looking down, saw two dirty boys, wearing clumsy breeches which were obviously cut down from grown-up trousers, coarse flannel shirts without collars, no stockings and heavy boots with broken and knotted laces.

"What are you doing up there?" said Dave.

"Go away!" said Alice. "Horrid boys, go away!"

"What's the matter, can't you get down?"

"'Course I can!" said Alice. Her foot slipped, and she clutched the tree-trunk desperately.

"Huh!" said Dave.

He sat down and began to take his boots off, eyeing Alice's neat, buttoned feet with contempt.

"You can't climb a tree in boots," he said.

"I know that!" said Alice, disgustedly.

Dave kicked his boots off and stood up. Alice looked enviously at his bare feet.

"If I take *my* boots off," she said, "I can't get them done up again without a button-hook."

Tommy sat with his arms round Pearl's neck, and watched admiringly while Dave climbed up the tree. It wasn't a very easy climb, and Dave was surprised that the girl had managed it—especially in boots. When he got near enough, he held out his hand.

"Come on," he said.

Alice didn't budge.

"I want my kite," she said.

Dave followed her gaze and saw the kite lodged in the tree above her.

"You don't want much, do you?" he said.

He had some trouble climbing past Alice and she had to move perilously along her branch to make room for him, but he managed it somehow. He reached up to free the bright blue and green kite. A twig snapped as he leaned forward.

"Be careful!" called Alice, alarmed.

Dave ignored her. He freed the kite and began to climb down with it again. Alice reached out for the kite.

"I'll bring it," said Dave. "You'd best get yourself down."

Alice scowled at him resentfully.

"Come on," said Dave, "give me your hand."

He tucked the kite under his arm and climbed on past Alice again, and then helped her down.

"Here's your kite," he said, when they were both safely on the ground.

"Thank you," said Alice, not very gratefully.

Tommy stood up, glowering at Alice. She glowered back at him.

"Why did you put your kite up in the tree?" inquired Tommy.

"I didn't do it on purpose!" said Alice. "I was trying to make it fly. But I can't run fast enough to get it up in the air."

"Dave could," said Tommy, loyally.

There is nothing in the world quite so companionable as flying a kite. It takes three people—one to run in front, pulling the string, another to run behind with the kite held as high as short arms will reach, and a third to run alongside shouting encouragement. "Now! Now!" The string feels the tug of the newly released kite. It swerves, it rises, dips, rises again—it is flying! It is flying . . . oh! It plunges to the ground like a wounded bird. Its three attendants race towards it, feeling all the anguish of their own lost wings. (For, surely, once upon a time, all men could fly?) Is the kite damaged? No. Its fragile framework is still firm, its brightly colored paper shows no rent. They smooth its tail, like a bird's feathers, and climb to a higher slope where the wind, instead of gusting treacherously, blows with a quiet, determined hum. Now.

"Run, Dave, run!"

"Hold it higher, Alice! Hold it higher! Now let it go!"

The kite rose, dipped, rose again. Dave ran faster and faster, and then turned and tugged, and felt the kite tug back, as though it said, "I am here! I am alive!" He eased the string, pulled it, eased it again. It was like playing a fish, except that a fishing-line robbed the fish of its liberty, but this string gave freedom to the kite. And as he released the string for the second time, he felt the kite take to the air with a strong, soaring motion. He was no longer in command. It was the kite which triumphantly demanded, and he obeyed, as the string ran through his fingers and the kite rose like a skylark into the limitless blue sky.

"Let me!" cried Alice. "Oh, let me!"

Dave readily made room for her to grasp the wooden bar, but, because the kite was pulling strongly now, he kept hold of it, too, feeding the string out with his other hand, and as they stood together, gazing upwards, it was as though the kite shared with them both the ecstasy of its flight.

"If we had some bits of paper, we could send wishes up the string," said Alice.

But for Dave, as he pulled and laughed with Alice, something more important than paper wishes went winging up the string, something black and hard and angry which would never quite return to him again.

When they had each had a turn at holding and running with the kite (Tommy, of course, fell over, and nearly lost it altogether) Alice said reluctantly, "I suppose I ought to go back for lunch."

"Do you mean 'dinner'?" said Dave.

"We call it 'lunch,' " said Alice.

"We call it 'dinner,' " said Dave.

They looked at each other coldly, and, as Dave began to wind the string round the wooden handle, it was as though some kind of magic, too, was wound down with the kite. When the kite plunged at last to earth, it was Alice who ran to retrieve it, as though it belonged to *her* instead of being something which they had all shared so joyfully together.

They began to walk back through the heather towards Emsdale.

"Why aren't you in school?" inquired Alice.

"Why do you think?" said Dave. "Summer holidays."

"You're lucky," said Alice. "I've got a horrible governess coming, and she'll want me to stay indoors all day, doing lessons."

"What's a governess?" asked Tommy.

"She's a sort of teacher," said Dave, and then had a qualm and glanced at Alice. "Isn't she?"

Alice wrinkled her nose and shrugged.

"Why don't you go to school, like us?" asked Tommy.

"Because we go to a colliery school," said Dave, "and she's a *lady!*"

Alice caught the note of contempt in his voice.

"I'm not a lady!" she said, furiously.

Dave smiled.

"I'm not a lady! I'm not!" cried Alice, and gave him a shove.

Dave shoved her back. They stood glaring at each other, and then Alice gave Dave another shove. Tommy flew at Alice and butted her in the stomach, and she dropped the kite and clutched Dave and they all three rolled down the hill together.

"I'm not a lady!" shouted Alice, and scrambled to her knees and pummeled Dave.

Dave held her off as best he could, and to begin with, he was as angry as she was. Then he suddenly began to laugh.

"Eh!" he said. "Eh, that's enough! I believe you."

"What do you mean?" cried Alice, angrily.

"I believe you," said Dave. "Ladies don't fight."

And then Alice began to laugh, too, and rolled over on her back, and she and Dave lay side by side, laughing, while Tommy looked, puzzled, from one to the other, and then grinned his sunny grin.

Tommy carried the kite back to the hill above the Mine Manager's house, and when he held it out to Alice, she took it reluctantly, and looked at Dave.

"Will you be here after lunch—dinner, I mean?" she asked.

Dave grinned.

"I reckon so," he said.

The sun was going down when Dave, Alice and Tommy lay on their stomachs in the hiding-place above the pit-head, sharing the piece of lardy-cake which Violet Armstrong had baked that morning. Pearl panted beside them.

"This is our secret place—mine and Tommy's," said Dave. "You can come, too, if you like."

"Oh, thank you!" cried Alice, well understanding what a

compliment that was. She looked down with interest. "I wonder what it's like down in the pit," she said.

"Haven't you ever been down?" said Tommy. "We go down all the time."

"You can't," said Alice. "You're too young. Boys aren't allowed to work down the mines until they're fourteen."

"We don't work exactly," said Dave. "We help Bert with the ponies."

"Who's Bert?"

"He's the Horsekeeper."

"Eh, it's grand!" said Tommy. "They all know us, do the ponies, and we know them—Bluey and Soldier and Lion . . ."

"And Flash," said Dave.

"I wish *I* could see them," said Alice. "Oh!" She suddenly sat up, looking at Dave in dismay.

"What's the matter?"

"The ponies," said Alice.

"What about them?"

"My father said—he's going to bring in machinery. He said the ponies would have to go."

Luke was just sitting down to his tea—a chump chop, with potatoes and greens—as Dave banged the door open, and Tommy jostled in behind him.

"The ponies!" Tommy shouted.

Violet put the teapot on the table.

"You're late again," she said. "Go and wash your hands, and then sit down and have your tea."

"The ponies!" cried Tommy again.

"What about the ponies?" asked Luke.

Dave looked at Violet.

"They're going to get rid of them. They're going to put machinery in instead."

Violet and Luke looked at each other, quickly.

"What will become of the ponies?" said Tommy. "What will they do with them?"

Violet's voice was suddenly hard.

"What *can* they do with them? No one's going to pay for their keep if they can't work."

Dave glanced at Luke, and saw him flinch, as though Violet's words had hit him like a blow.

"Come on," said Violet. "Hurry up and wash and have your tea."

Tommy made a move towards the wash-house, but Dave stayed where he was, and looked directly at Luke.

"What will happen to them?" he asked.

"How should I know?" said Luke, harshly. "Be thankful if it's only the ponies they get rid of, and not the men!"

Dave stared at him. He had appealed to Luke, and Luke had let him down, just as he had let down his father too. All the subdued anger and bitterness which Dave felt boiled up and burst its bounds.

"Of course *you* wouldn't care!" said Dave. "You're the one that left my father in the pit. You got out yourself, and left him to die!"

Luke got up in one violent movement, and raised his arm.

"Luke!" cried Violet, a note of panic in her voice.

Luke looked at her, looked back at Dave and suddenly turned and snatched his cap from the peg, wrenched the door open and went out, banging it shut behind him. Pearl crept out to the wash-house.

Violet looked at Dave. He stared back at her defiantly.

"How could you!" said Violet. "Dave, how *could* you say that to him?"

She looked at the uneaten chop on Luke's plate.

"He hasn't even started his tea. He's been working hard all day down the pit, to keep us in food and clothes, and then you come in and—!"

"I don't care," said Dave. "He's no right to be here in our house."

"It's *his* house now," said Violet. "He works to keep it for all of us."

"I don't care," said Dave. "I don't want him here."

"Nor do I," said Tommy, faithfully.

"What does it matter what you want?" shouted Violet, suddenly losing her temper. "You can go up to bed. Both of you! You can go without your tea. Perhaps that'll teach you to remember who earns it for you!"

Tommy, alarmed, went quickly up the narrow flight of stairs which led straight out of the kitchen, and Dave followed him more slowly. He glanced back and saw his mother putting an enamel plate over Luke's tea to keep it warm on the stove, and he scowled.

Dave and Tommy slept in a tiny room at the back of the house. It had a sloping roof, and there was just room in it for one bed and a small wooden chair.

"Don't cry, Tom," said Dave. "It was me she was cross with."

Tommy sniffed dolefully.

"I want me tea," he said, always one for concentrating his mind on essentials.

"What're you fussing about? You had your lardy-cake."

"Alice had half of it!" said Tommy, bitterly.

Dave's sympathy suddenly ran out.

"Oh, get undressed and get into bed," he said, "unless you want to make her crosser."

Tommy grizzled himself to sleep quite soon, but Dave lay on his back, watching the light slowly fade and listening to the sounds from the village. He could hear men's voices from the pub and the uneven "oompa-ing" noise of the Colliery Band practicing in the back room. After some time, he heard heavy boots on the cobblestones, and the men calling good night to each other from their front doors.

It was quite dark except for the moon when he heard footsteps on the stairs. The door opened, and his mother came in, carrying a bowl.

"I brought you some bread and milk," she said.

She gave him the bowl, and sat down by the bed. Dave looked at Tommy, and saw his mother smile in the dim light.

"If he's asleep, you can eat it all," she said.

It was wonderful to sit and eat the bread and milk all alone with his mother, except for Tommy sleeping beside him. He had nearly finished when Violet said, hesitating, "Dave—you know Luke didn't leave your father."

"Yes, he did," said Dave.

"No, he didn't. Luke was injured in the fall and your father went in to rescue him. Then there was—the second explosion."

"I know," said Dave. "But Luke could've . . ." he stopped. "He could have done *something*."

"He was brought out unconscious!" said Violet. "What *could* he do?"

Dave didn't answer. He finished the bread and milk and avoided her eyes. Violet stood up and took the bowl.

"Come on," she said. "You'd best tuck down now."

She pulled the bedclothes over him, and bent down to kiss him.

"Good night," she said. "God bless."

Her light footsteps crossed the wooden floor, and then she paused.

"Dave," she said.

Dave looked up, and saw his mother smiling in the doorway.

"I shouldn't worry too much about the ponies," she said. "Luke was talking to Sam Carter in the pub. Sam says, no matter what the Manager says, His Lordship will never spend that much—not on machines!"

CHAPTER SIX

MR. Sandman spread the plans and diagrams out on Lord Harrogate's desk.

"This is what I would suggest, my Lord—a main-and-tail hauler. The engine would be installed here, near the main shaft, and then . . ."

Lord Harrogate's attention had been caught by a pamphlet of mining machinery, and he picked it up.

"What is this?" he inquired.

"That is a coal-cutting machine, my Lord."

"Splendid!" cried Lord Harrogate. "Let's get some of those, too."

Mr. Sandman hesitated.

"Well, yes, my Lord," he said. "They might be of use in certain areas of the pit, but we have to consider whether the cost will be justified by the resulting return in improved . . ."

Lord Harrogate looked up at him. A rather unfriendly glint had come into his eye, like a lion who has been offered a large bone and now sees it being removed from his grasp.

"What's that?" he said, sharply. "Aren't they any good, these machines? I thought you said—"

"Oh certainly, my Lord!" replied Sandman hastily. "I have gone into the matter very carefully. I am sure that machinery is the answer. It is just that you will want to be assured of a reasonable return on any investment which you may make."

"Hm?" said Lord Harrogate. "What? If we install this machinery, I shall expect the colliery to make money, of course."

"Yes, my Lord," said Sandman. "That certainly should be the result." He paused. His conscience compelled him to qualify this statement. "It may take a year or two, but by getting a greater quantity of coal out at a lower cost, and by making better use of the labor which is at present employed . . ."

But Lord Harrogate was no longer listening. His interest had wandered to a loud humming noise coming from the hall.

"I do believe—!" he exclaimed. He leaped to his feet, went to the door and listened. "By Jove!" he cried. "Yes! Yes, indeed! Come along, my dear Sanderson. This will interest you."

And he flung the door open and vanished out into the hall. Trying to get his wits together, Mr. Sanderson followed him, and found the owner gazing with rapture at a large and unwieldy machine rather like an inefficient bellows. It was attached to a thick hose, with which a nervous housemaid seemed to be attempting to sweep the carpet.

"Ah, well done, Ellen!" cried Lord Harrogate. "Well done, indeed! You see, Sanders, they used to have to sweep all the carpets by hand. But then I bought this machine— the very latest thing—it's called a vacuum cleaner."

"I see, my Lord," said Sandman. "Yes."

The machine really was making the most extraordinary noise.

"You see," said Lord Harrogate, "it just sucks all the dust up out of the carpet, and—"

The machine began to pump a great deal faster than before, hesitated, coughed and deposited a huge pile of nasty-looking gray dust and fluff on the carpet. Ellen looked at Lord Harrogate.

"My dear girl," exclaimed Lord Harrogate in astonishment, "how did you manage to do that?" He turned to

Sandman and spoke in an aside which reverberated round the marble hall. "She hasn't quite got the hang of it yet," he said.

He turned blithely away. Mr. Sandman realized with some alarm that Lord Harrogate was heading, not for the study and a renewed perusal of the plans and diagrams, but for the conservatory.

"Er—my Lord!" he called.

Lord Harrogate paused.

"Eh? What?"

"About the machinery, my Lord, for the colliery?"

Lord Harrogate looked surprised. He seemed to have forgotten all about it.

"Machinery?" he said. "Oh yes. Certainly. Get all the machinery you need."

A footman opened the door, and Lord Harrogate vanished into the conservatory. By the time Mr. Sandman had retrieved his papers from the study and was again passing through the hall to take his hat from the butler, Ellen was on her hands and knees, dourly sweeping up the dust and fluff with a dustpan and brush.

"Those are the engineers from Sheffield," said Dave.

He and Alice and Tommy were in their hiding-place, looking down into the pit-head. Big crates were being unloaded from the railway trucks, and a man in a black suit with a gold watch-chain was talking to Mr. Sandman outside his offices.

"How long will they take to install it?" asked Alice.

"Don't know. Bert says they're going to lay electric cables first."

"And won't they use any ponies in the pit at all?"

Dave shook his head.

"Bert says they might have done, just to haul the tubs from the face to the machine in the main roadway. But ours is just a small pit, and so the Manager—" he paused, and Alice looked at him quickly "—your father reckons they can manhandle them."

Alice sighed.

"I wish I could go down and see them working, and the stables and everything, while they're still there."

"Well, you can't," said Tommy, with some satisfaction. "Girls aren't allowed down the pit."

"Nor are boys," said Alice, "but *you* get down. And I'm

bigger than you are." She stopped short, and eyed Tommy in a measuring sort of way. "But not much," she said.

Alice looked at Dave. His mouth came open.

"No! Alice! You can't! No!"

Twenty minutes later, Bert, moving towards the cage with the maintenance workers, was joined by Dave, accompanied by a smaller figure in a large cloth-cap and Tommy's overcoat, cut down by Violet from an old one of their father's, no stockings and clumsy, ill-fitting boots. Bert glanced carelessly at Dave, and at the cloth-cap, which was about all he could see of the smaller figure. He took his disc from the tally-man, and jerked his head towards the boys.

"Got any spares?" he inquired.

The tally-man glanced at Dave and at the cloth-cap, and handed out two discs. Dave took them both, and hung one round his neck and gave the other to a small and rather clean hand emerging from the ragged overcoat, and they all three jostled into the cage.

Mr. Sandman, standing beside the desk in his office, saw the two smaller figures mingling with the maintenance workers and the emerging miners. He went quickly to the door, and out on to the iron passageway overlooking the yard. He started down the steps to stop the boys going down, but, as he reached the bottom, he realized that it was too late. The cage door was shut, and the cage was already sinking down.

"Carter!" called Mr. Sandman.

Sam Carter had been talking to a group of miners, and turned away, smiling, but the smile faded as soon as he saw Mr. Sandman's face.

"If I see those boys going down again," said Mr. Sandman, "you'll be dismissed!"

The wind roared and rushed round the cage, and the wet bricks of the shaft lining flashed upwards. Bert, glancing idly down, saw beneath the cloth-cap Alice's face, full of glee and excitement. Aghast, Bert looked at Dave, looked again at Alice and moved quickly between her and the other men in the cage. Dave nudged Alice, and she lowered her head again. Tense but triumphant, she knew for the first time what only miners know—that beneath the surface of the earth there is another secret world, silent except for the constant dripping of water, and, away from the lights at the pit-bottom, so dark that the blackness seems to press upon the eyeballs. The miner, tunneling through the solid earth, makes this secret world his own. He explores it, but never conquers it, and those who venture into it with him must know for a few moments the dangers which he accepts all his life.

As soon as they reached the pit-bottom, Bert hustled Dave and Alice along the passage. Dave hadn't wanted Alice to come down, but he couldn't help being pleased and proud at her delight when she saw the stables, and the ponies of whom she had heard so much.

"This is Bluey," he said, "and Soldier and Lion—and this is Flash."

"Flash!" cried Alice. "Oh, Flash, *darling!*"

"Eh, watch it!" said Dave. "He's not used to strangers."

But Alice had put her arms round Flash's neck, and her face down on his absurd parti-colored top-knot, and Flash didn't seem to mind at all.

"Shall I take his bridle off?" asked Alice.

"You might as well," Dave replied, half-jealous, half-pleased.

Alice was used to helping to groom her father's horse, and had even learned to ride on the old cob which they had left behind in Kent, so she proved to be quite useful in feeding and grooming the ponies. In fact, she was more useful than Tommy, whose attention was apt to wander, and whose small fingers could not always manage the stiff leather and buckles.

"Did you see the machinery on top?" asked Bert.

"Machinery?" said Dave quickly.

"Them big crates."

"Oh. Yes."

Bert put some fodder in Flash's feeding-basket, and patted his neck.

"Poor beasts," he said. "They won't be here much longer."

"Why do you call them that?" asked Alice, astonished.

Bert looked at her with equal astonishment.

"Why," he said, "there'll be no place for them in the pit."

"I know, but that's good, really."

"Oh, aye?" said Bert.

Alice's brown eyes were glowing with pleasure.

"If there's no work for them, they'll be brought up out of the mine, and let out into the fields. We can visit them every day, and feed them and look after them—Flash, and

Soldier and Lion and—and all of them! And they'll be able
to run about in the sunshine and be happy and safe for the
rest of their lives!"

Alice smiled at Dave and he, caught up by her enthusiasm, suddenly smiled back.

"That's what you think, is it?" said Bert.

They both looked quickly at Bert. Bert's eyes were fixed
on Alice.

"Ask thy father," he said. "Ask thy father what will become of pit ponies!"

Restored to her navy-blue coat with the brass buttons,
which Tommy was only too thankful to relinquish, Alice
raced down the hill towards the house. She slammed
through the garden gate, wrenched open the front door and
banged it behind her.

"Father!" she called.

She opened the drawing-room door.

"Father?"

Inside the door was a tall lady dressed all in black. Mrs.
Sandman rose from her chair by the fire.

"Alice, dear, Alice!" she said. "This is Miss Coutts. She
has come to be your Governess."

CHAPTER SEVEN

Miss Coutts had a bundle of slightly frizzy, mousy hair,
and pale blue eyes in a sharp, pale face.

"Had you forgotten that Miss Coutts was arriving today?" asked Mrs. Sandman, nervously.

Alice said nothing. She had been well aware that the
Governess was coming, and had taken care to keep out of

the way all afternoon, but then, in the excitement of going down the pit, she had forgotten. Otherwise she would have washed off some of the coal-dust before coming into the drawing-room. Miss Coutts extended a long, black-gloved hand.

"How do you do, Alice?" she said.

She gave Alice a limp handshake, and then surveyed her with a neat smile which did not get beyond her small, sharp teeth.

"Dear me!" she exclaimed. "We *are* a Miss Grubby-Paws, aren't we?"

"I'm afraid we have rather—let her run wild," said Mrs. Sandman, anxiously.

"Never mind, Mrs. Sandman," said Miss Coutts, with a grim touch of cheeriness in her voice, "I'm sure we shall soon get Alice back into *ladylike* ways again."

This was not an ambition which Alice could applaud, but she had other things on her mind at the moment.

"Mother," she said, "when will Father be home? I want to ask him—"

"Alice, dear, Alice!" cried Mrs. Sandman, hastily answering a disapproving look from Miss Coutts. "Where are your manners? Miss Coutts was just going upstairs. You may go with her and show her the schoolroom."

Alice, going upstairs ahead of Miss Coutts, was uneasily conscious of her half-buttoned boots. She opened the schoolroom door, and Miss Coutts surveyed the small, square room, with its low window looking out over the moors.

"Hmm," she said. "Not a very *large* room, is it?"

Alice scowled resentfully. She knew how much trouble her mother and Clara had taken to make the room look nice, polishing the table, and putting a vase of flowers on the window-sill.

"Never mind," said Miss Coutts. "You know what they say—'little and good.'" She peered hopefully down at Alice from under her large black hat. "I think we're going to get on very well together, don't you?"

Alice could not bring herself to lie, but she forced a smile, and Miss Coutts seemed quite satisfied.

"Tomorrow morning," she said, "before we do anything else, we will sit down together and make out a timetable, so that we can make good use of our time from morning to night. 'Every moment is lent; every moment must be well spent.' That must be our motto."

Alice looked at her, dismayed. She thought she had never heard a more unattractive proposition. Miss Coutts turned brightly towards the door.

"Now, it's off to Bedfordshire for you," she said. "But first, a nice bath."

"Yes, Miss Coutts," said Alice. She was obliged to admit that she really did need a bath.

"Remember, Alice," said Miss Coutts, earnestly, "a little lady is clean and neat at all times."

"Yes, Miss Coutts," said Alice, gloomily.

It was a relief when Mrs. Sandman came as usual to say good night, and Alice eagerly sat up in bed.

"Mother," she said, "is Father home?"

"No, dear, not yet. He's working late at the colliery. The new machinery is a big responsibility to him."

"But, Mother, I wanted to ask him——"

"Now, Alice, go to sleep, there's a good girl."

Alice lay awake for a long time, waiting for the sound of the front door, and for her father to come upstairs, as he always did, to kiss her good night. But the last of the light faded and he still had not come. At last she fell asleep, and dreamed of the ponies running free in the green fields—Flash and Bluey and Soldier and Lion and all the others—while she and Dave and Tommy ran beside them, laughing.

But when she awoke in the morning, she felt dreadfully unhappy and worried. At first she thought it was because Miss Coutts had come, with her awful timetable of lessons and crochet and pianoforte, but then she remembered the ponies. She dressed in a hurry, and thumped down the stairs three at a time and burst into the dining-room. At the end of the table was an egg-shell and an empty coffee cup and a plate with toast-crumbs on it. She was too late. Her father was not there.

Miss Coutts was at the sideboard, helping herself from the silver-plated chafing-dish, and Mrs. Sandman was pouring coffee at the table.

"Mother," began Alice, "do you know if——?"

"Alice, dear," Miss Coutts interrupted, "aren't you going to say 'good morning'?"

"Good morning," said Alice, and took a hasty breath to continue.

"And to your Mama?" prompted Miss Coutts.

"Good morning, Mother."

"Good morning, Alice," said Mrs. Sandman. She seemed nervous. Perhaps she was wondering if Miss Coutts would think that "Mama" was more genteel than "Mother."

"Sit down, dear," said Miss Coutts. "Shall I help you to some bacon and eggs?"

"No, thank you," said Alice. "Clara brings me some porridge. Mother, do you know if Father's left yet?"

"Yes, dear," said Mrs. Sandman. "He had his breakfast early, and went to the—to the colliery."

She glanced at Miss Coutts as she said the word. Alice had a notion that Miss Coutts had made it clear that she thought that a colliery was rather a vulgar place.

The Governess returned to her place with a plate piled high with bacon, eggs, sausages and mushrooms, as Clara came cheerfully in.

"Thump, thump, thump, Miss Alice!" she said. "I always know when you've come downstairs!"

She banged the bowl of porridge down in front of Alice, and they grinned at each other. Mrs. Sandman caught Miss Coutts' disapproving look.

"That will do, Clara," said Mrs. Sandman, in a chilly tone.

Clara was offended.

"Yes, Mum," she said, and went out and closed the door so hard that it was almost a bang.

Mrs. Sandman smiled deprecatingly at Miss Coutts.

"I'm afraid," she said, "that when you have to employ local servants, they do tend to become rather familiar."

"Ye-es," said Miss Coutts. Her tone seemed to indicate that this would not happen in *her* household. "My dear father used to say," she added, "that the kindest task we could perform for the lower orders was to teach them to know their place and to keep it."

"Oh *yes!*" said Mrs. Sandman, wistfully.

Carefully buttering a piece of toast, Miss Coutts pursued her undoubted advantage.

"I notice," she said, "that Alice has picked up quite a Yorkshire accent."

"Really?" said Mrs. Sandman, dismayed. "I can't think how that has happened. She never plays with any of the local children."

"I should hope not, indeed!" cried Miss Coutts, with a pitying smile. "But perhaps she had been spending just a *leetle* too much time with the servants."

And, picking up her knife and fork, she began to eat her breakfast with relish. Alice saw her chance.

"Mother," she said, "I must see Father. Do you know if he—?"

"Now, Alice," said Mrs. Sandman, "you mustn't bother him. He has a lot on his mind."

"Yes, but—"

"And you know," said Miss Coutts, "little girls should be seen and not heard."

"But I must *ask* him something!" said Alice, desperately.

Miss Coutts put down her knife and fork with the air of one determined to do her duty at all costs.

"Well, Alice," she said, "perhaps *I* can tell you what you want to know."

Alice hesitated. It seemed unlikely, but, after all, Miss Coutts was a governess, and governesses were supposed to know things.

"It's about the ponies," she said.

"Ponies?" repeated Miss Coutts, blankly.

"The pit ponies. Father's bringing machinery into the mine, to do the work the ponies used to do. I want to know what will happen to them."

"Well, dear," said Miss Coutts, after a quick glance at Mrs. Sandman, "I suppose, if their usefulness is finished, they'll have to go."

"But—go *where?*" Alice demanded.

When Miss Coutts did not reply at once, she turned to Mrs. Sandman.

"Mother?"

"Well, I suppose," Mrs. Sandman looked helplessly at Miss Coutts, "I really don't . . . That is, I'm sure your father will have made plans for them."

"But, *what* plans?" Alice persisted. "What will become of them?"

Mrs. Sandman looked at Miss Coutts, and Alice followed her gaze.

"Well," said Miss Coutts, obviously thinking that she must come up with something, "if there's no work for them to do, I imagine they'll be sent—er . . ." she paused.

"Sent where?" asked Alice.

Miss Coutts smiled, happy to have found an answer at last.

"To the slaughter-house, dear, I imagine."

Alice stared at her, horrified.

"No!" she said. "No! Father wouldn't do a thing like that!"

She flung down her spoon and rushed to the door.

"Alice!" called Miss Coutts, astonished.

But Alice had gone, running straight through the hall and out of the front door and setting off down the hill towards the colliery.

In the Mine Manager's office, Mr. Sandman was staring indignantly at the Chief Engineer.

"Close the pit?" he said.

"Only while we're laying the cables," said the Engineer.

"It's out of the question," replied Mr. Sandman. "If I stopped production during the installation, it would take months to make up the loss. I'm going to have a difficult enough time trying to recoup the cost of the machinery."

The Engineer shrugged. A single-minded man, he would have laid cables and installed machinery in Hell if the Devil had asked him, and his only interest in the tortures of the damned would have been to request that they should not interfere with his men's work.

"Well, it's your choice," he said. He went to the door and opened it. "But my men are working under great difficulties—and the pit-men don't go out of their way to make it any easier."

Sam Carter came in at that moment, and stood aside to allow the Engineer to go out, with a hostile look which seemed to confirm his words.

"We've had to stop work in the lower drift heading," he said.

"What?" exclaimed Mr. Sandman. "Why?"

"They can't work while that cable's being laid," said Sam. "It's not safe to drive the ponies, with bales of wire and all them strangers about. We've had one runner already."

"A runner!" said Mr. Sandman, sharply.

He knew all too well what a runner was—a runaway pony, clattering on iron hooves along the dark, narrow passage with that lethal load of iron and timber which could crush or kill anything in its path.

"Was anyone hurt?"

"Not this time," replied Sam, grimly. "But I've told the men to stop work."

Alice arrived, breathless, in the doorway.

"Hullo, Missy," said Sam.

Sandman glanced at her, irritated.

"Alice," he said. "What are you doing here?"

"I wanted to ask you something," said Alice.

Mr. Sandman forced himself to speak kindly.

"Not now, dear," he said. "I'm busy. You run along."

He spread a plan out on his desk.

"The lower drift heading," he said. "And they're laying the cable here?"

Sam Carter came to look.

"That's right."

Mr. Sandman bit his thumb and frowned.

"Yes. Yes, I see."

On one side was the loss of money for the colliery and wages for the men; on the other side was the dread of every Mine Manager—a serious accident in the pit.

"Shall I send the men home, then?" asked Sam Carter.

Mr. Sandman made up his mind.

"Yes," he said. "Send them home."

He was aware—much more aware than the men would have believed—that the loss of a day's or a week's wages might mean children going hungry or barefoot, but the decision was his, and he must make it, right or wrong, and then sleep with it that night.

Sam Carter nodded and went out. Sandman saw Alice, still waiting.

"Alice," he said, irritated. "Are you still here? What do you want?"

"It's about the ponies, Father," said Alice.

"The ponies?"

"Yes. What will become of them?"

"Well, really, Alice," said Sandman, taken by surprise, "really, I . . ."

"Please, Father."

A slight uneasiness crept into Mr. Sandman's voice.

"We can hardly turn them loose on the moors," he said. "They're not accustomed to fend for themselves."

"Isn't there a field somewhere, where they can live happily and run about and—and—?"

"Who would look after them? You can't just turn them out in a field to starve. Who would pay for their feed?"

"The colliery!" cried Alice. "They work in the pit!"

Mr. Sandman's eye had wandered towards the work-schedule on his desk. He looked back at her, exasperated.

"Really, Alice," he said, "it's out of the question! You could hardly expect Lord Harrogate to pay for animals to do nothing, any more than men!"

"Well, then," Alice persisted, "what *will* become of them?"

She saw her father hesitate.

"They won't be sent to the slaughter-house," she said, "will they?"

She saw the truth in his face.

"Father?" she demanded incredulously.

Worried and uneasy, Mr. Sandman suddenly lost his temper.

"Now, Alice, run along!" he said. "Why aren't you with your Governess? I've got enough on my mind, without being bothered about a lot of ponies!"

Alice stared at him, aghast, and then turned and ran out of the office.

Mr. Sandman immediately regretted his impatience. He took a step after her.

"Alice!"

He went to the door, and saw the small figure running blindly across the yard.

"Alice?"

But she had scrambled through the fence and up the hill, and vanished. Mr. Sandman turned back into his office. He sat down at his desk, and sighed. It was the first time that his daughter had asked for his help, and he had refused it, and it made him very unhappy. But, at the same time, because he felt guilty, something inside him hardened as well.

CHAPTER EIGHT

UP on the moors, Dave and Tommy were squatting in the heather, putting little trails of grain and raisins along the sandy track.

"Eh, don't chuck it about!" said Dave. "Put the grain along there. The birds'll run along that little path, and straight into Bert's snare."

"But there isn't any snare," said Tommy.

"Nay, but it will be. We're just baiting the path, to get the birds used to coming here. Then Bert'll put a snare there—a wire loop under the heather—and the pheasants'll run right into it."

"I think that's cruel," said Tommy.

He was not a boy of acute sensibilities, but even he could feel for a pheasant lured to its death by delicious and deceitful food.

Dave grinned at him.

"Maybe it is," he said, "but when Bert fetches up at the back door and gives Mum a brace of pheasants, I don't notice you refusing to eat *your* share! Anyway, life *is* cruel, didn't you know?"

With a sudden, heart-stopping whir and clatter, a covey of partridges flew up out of the heather behind them, and the boys turned and saw Alice stumbling towards them. Her hair had escaped from its ribbon, and she was almost blind with crying, the tears still streaming down her face.

"Alice!" called Dave. "What is it? What's the matter?"

"The ponies!" she said. "My father—he's going to kill them!"

And she fell down in the heather beside them, and sobbed as if her heart would break.

Dave looked at her, horrified. "Kill them?" How could anyone kill the ponies? Dreadful pictures invaded his mind and eyes—of Flash and Bluey being beaten and bludgeoned about the head, and staggering about on their little hooves, and falling in pools of blood. He found it difficult to speak, but he had to know more.

"How?" he said. "What will they—?"

Alice raised her head and gasped through her tears, "He's going to send them to the slaughter-house!"

Dave had never been to a slaughter-house, but he had seen cattle and sheep being driven off to market, and it brought new nightmare visions of Flash, sturdy, independent, heroically loyal Flash, being hustled into a truck, and clattering about, frightened and helpless, with no more dignity than a squawking hen. He knew that Alice was seeing the same horrifying images as he was, and she put her face down on her arms again, sobbing, "Father, oh, Father!" as though what would be done to the ponies was not more horrible than the fact that it was her father who would be doing it.

Tommy was of an age and nature where he found it hard to imagine unfamiliar things, whether good or bad, so he was less touched by the ponies' imagined sufferings than by Alice's real and apparent grief. He put a grubby hand on her shoulder.

"Don't cry, Alice," he said. "Dave'll think of something."

His words penetrated Alice's sorrow. She had almost cried herself out, anyway. She raised her head again, and looked at Dave.

"Will you? Is there something we can do to save them? Is there really?"

Dave realized with some alarm that both Tommy and Alice were gazing at him expectantly.

And then it came to him with blinding certainty. "Yes," he said. "There's only one thing to do. We'll steal them up out of the pit, and take them somewhere, and keep them safe."

It only took Alice a second to think it over, and be as convinced as he was.

"Oh yes!" she cried. "Of course! That's what we must do!"

And Tommy beamed, too.

"How will we do it?" asked Alice.

"Well . . ." said Dave. They were looking at him again, and he had absolutely no idea. Inspiration came, and he finished with relief, "We'll ask Bert. He'll know the best way to do it."

"I'd better go," said Alice. "I'm supposed to be doing lessons with the Governess."

"Wait till we've done this, and we'll walk back with you," said Dave.

The boys finished laying the bait for Bert's snares. It was poaching, of course, because all the moors round there belonged to Lord Harrogate or to Lord Kirkdale (which was how they came to own the coal-mines underneath them), and the game-birds on the moors were supposed to belong to them as well. But, as Bert said, "What the eye doesn't see, the heart doesn't grieve over," and he'd never been caught yet.

"You'll come and tell me what Bert says, won't you?" said Alice, as they walked back towards Emsdale.

"Aye," said Dave, "but by the time we get up tonight, most likely it'll be too late."

"Tomorrow morning, then," said Alice. "If you wait outside the gate, I'll come out directly after breakfast."

"If you can get away from the Governess," said Dave.

Alice grinned. Like the others, she was feeling marvelously elated, as though the ponies were already rescued.

"I can run faster than she can," she said.

When the boys went up to the pit-head that evening, they saw Luke talking to Sam Carter. Luke's team was one of those which had been laid off because of the engineers.

"Any work for me and my mate tomorrow, Sam?" he asked.

"Can't say, Luke," Sam answered. "Better come tomorrow and see what the chances are."

Luke scowled and turned away.

"Eh, Luke!" called Sam.

Luke paused.

"I reckon they'll finish laying the cables in the main roadway tonight. Most like you'll be able to go on shift tomorrow."

Luke nodded and gave him one of his reluctant smiles.

Sam Carter, turning away, saw Dave and Tommy hurrying towards the pit-head.

"Dave! Tommy!" he called. "You can't go down, lads!"

They looked at him in astonishment.

"But, Sam," said Dave, "we always help Bert."

"Maybe so, but you can't do it no more. The Manager won't have it."

"He won't know. Please, Sam."

"Nay, lad," said Sam Carter. "It's more than my job's worth." He began to turn away, but then paused. "And don't try to slip down when I'm not here, because if you do, it's Luke as'll get the blame."

Dave glanced after the tall figure of Luke just going through the big gates.

"It's nothing to do with him!"

"No?" said Sam. "What would become of you if Luke lost his place? You'd be clemmed and homeless, lad. Think on."

Dave was scowling as he walked along the village street, with Tommy trudging along beside him. Tommy glanced up at him nervously.

"Bert will help us to get them out," he said.

Dave turned on him.

"You're not to speak of it to Bert, you hear?"

"Why not, Dave? He'd help us."

"He might tell Luke," said Dave.

"Luke—" began Tommy, and then stopped. He kicked the dust with the toe of his boot, and finished in a mumble. "Luke likes the ponies. He might help us."

"Huh!" said Dave, with contempt. "Not him! He'd be afraid of losing his *place!*"

He walked on, and Tommy hurried after him, troubled and confused.

As they went into the kitchen, Luke was sitting in the old armchair by the fire, lighting his pipe. Violet was in the wash-house, cleaning Luke's miner's lamp.

"Where have you been?" she asked, as the boys came through.

"Out on the moors."

She looked carefully at the lamp, and, satisfied, put it down on the newspaper on top of the copper and turned to go into the kitchen.

"Your tea's in the oven. Wash your hands, and then come and sit down."

Tommy looked up at Dave as Dave pumped the water into the sink.

"If we can't get into the pit," he said, "how can we get the ponies out?"

"Oh, wash thee hands and howd thee gob," said Dave, and pumped ferociously on, his face troubled.

After breakfast next morning, Alice hung over the back gate while Dave and Tommy squatted down behind the stone wall.

"Can't we just go along at night," said Alice, "and wind them up in the cage?"

Dave shook his head.

"Someone would hear us. Besides, there are always people about—doing maintenance and that."

"But then, how *can* we get them up? Unless there's another way in . . ."

"There might be some old workings," said Dave. "If we could get down into them, and find our way through."

"How do we know where they are?"

"Oh," said Dave, "they always keep plans of all the workings."

"Alice!" called Miss Coutts from the house.

Dave, who had stood up in his excitement at the new thought, hastily bobbed down again. Alice glanced over her shoulder, and saw Miss Coutts in the doorway.

"Where?" she asked urgently. "Where do they keep the plans?"

She saw Dave grin and then she heard Miss Coutts' footsteps on the path and hastily turned away.

"In thy father's office," said Dave, behind her.

CHAPTER NINE

THE little schoolroom was very stuffy as Alice sat at the table that afternoon, looking wistfully out of the window. In obedience to the timetable which Miss Coutts had prepared, all green, blue and purple ink, she had been in there all day, except for lunchtime, and even then Miss Coutts had endeavored to improve her mind with little homilies about ladylike table-manners and polite subjects of conversation. Now Miss Coutts, with frequent recourse to a rather highly colored *Child's Guide to the Kings and Queens of England,* was correcting Alice's history exercise.

"Alice," she said, "why have you left out the Plantagenets?"

"Plantagenets?" replied Alice, vaguely.

If she leaned a little to the right, she could just see the big black wheels turning above the pit.

"Surely," said Miss Coutts, reproachfully, "you haven't forgotten the Little Princes in the Tower?"

"Oh," said Alice.

"Edward the Fifth," said Miss Coutts, with a sentimental sigh. "You must remember that dear little boy."

Alice returned her attention from the window to Miss Coutts.

"You don't *know* he was a dear little boy," she remarked. "He might have been a horrid little boy, even if he *was* a King. There might be common little boys who were much nicer."

"Ye-es," said Miss Coutts, doubtfully. "Of course, 'kind

hearts are more than coronets', but still—I think we can say that breeding tells."

The clock on the mantelpiece struck four. Alice leaped to her feet.

"Can I go now?"

"Oh," said Miss Coutts, taken by surprise, "well, lessons are over, but . . ."

Alice had opened the door.

"I thought I'd go for a walk," she said, and was through the door in a flash.

"Alice!" cried Miss Coutts, getting up and hurrying to the door.

Alice was already leaping down the stairs with a series of resounding thumps.

"It's nearly time for tea!" Miss Coutts called over the banisters.

"I'll take it with me!" Alice shouted, and vanished into the kitchen.

Clara was cutting thin bread and butter, and Mrs. Green was taking her newly baked rock-cakes out of the oven. Alice, darting in, paused, sniffing.

"Mm, can I have one, Mrs. Green?"

Without waiting for an answer, she picked one up and set off for the back door.

"Now then, Miss Alice!" said Mrs. Green, but she never minded what Alice did.

Alice began to eat the rock-cake, which crumbled deliciously.

"*Mm!*" she said again, and returned to pick up several more, before rushing out, with a parting grin at Clara.

"There now!" exclaimed Mrs. Green, gazing at the depleted baking-tin, "I suppose I'd better bake some more. That there Governess eats like a h'Elephant at the Zoo."

Clutching the rock-cakes in her pinafore, Alice raced through the garden and out of the gate. At the schoolroom window lurked Miss Coutts, peering out, with a puzzled expression. Were there sheep beyond the stone wall, or was it two heads which she had seen bobbing down as Alice emerged?

At the pit-head, Sam Carter and the Chief Engineer had almost come to blows.

"You're not taking that down!" roared Sam.

"What do you mean?"

"That's welding equipment!"

The miners standing about in the yard looked at each other quickly.

"What about it?" demanded the Engineer.

"You're not taking that down!" repeated Sam, still more loudly.

"The Manager said we were to carry on with——"

"Carry on like that, and you'll blow the whole pit up!" said Sam.

Mr. Sandman, hearing the ruckus, came out of his office.

"What's going on, Carter?"

He did not see Alice, Dave and Tommy, crouching under the iron staircase, as he descended the steps into the yard and went towards the indignant disputants. Sam Carter came to meet him.

"You'd better come, sir, unless you want the whole pit idle!"

"What?" exclaimed Mr. Sandman, and walked with him towards the pit-head.

"Now!" said Dave, and Alice darted up the steps and into the office.

It was disconcerting to find that the office was full of plans—pinned to the walls, spread out on the desk and rolled up in every corner. At first, Alice was so afraid that her father would come back and find her there, that she grabbed the first one she could see and was ready to settle for that. But as she unrolled it, she saw at the bottom, in Mr. Sandman's copperplate handwriting, "Present Workings, 1909." She peeped through the window. Her father seemed to be deep in argument with the Engineer. She looked round the room. On the far side was a cabinet, like the chest in which her cousin kept his collection of birds' eggs. Alice pulled down the brass ring on the bottom drawer. A shower of rolled plans cascaded on to the floor.

"Any welding which is to be done will be done on the surface," said Mr. Sandman. "Is that understood?"

The Chief Engineer nodded, and Mr. Sandman turned back towards his office. Dave and Tommy looked at each other, alarmed, and then towards the top of the staircase, but there was no sign of Alice. She was on her knees, diligently going through the rolls of maps, in search of the right one.

"I suppose you realize," said the Chief Engineer, "that it'll set the installation back by two weeks?"

Mr. Sandman stopped dead in his tracks. He turned back.

"I realize no such thing. That is absolutely absurd. I shall send for your Managing Director from Sheffield!"

He turned once more towards the office.

"Where *is* she?" said Dave, looking anxiously towards the window. Alice had just found a map dated some years earlier, with an inscription "Disused Workings" written in the former Manager's crabbed handwriting. Dave and Tommy shrank back into the long grass under the staircase as Mr. Sandman walked steadily towards them.

"Er—just a minute," said the Chief Engineer behind him. "I daresay we can work something out."

Mr. Sandman stood still for a moment, before turning to confront the man.

"Oh?" he said, coldly.

Sam Carter's lips twitched, and he glanced at Mr. Sandman with the first tiny sign of admiration he had yet shown him.

"Well . . ." said the Engineer, uneasily.

Mr. Sandman gave him his full attention.

"I am certainly not prepared to accept any delay in the installation," he said. "What do you suggest?"

Alice had thrust the remaining plans back in the cabinet. She crept to the door with the one showing the old workings, and threw an anxious glance at the group by the pit-head. Her heart in her mouth, she dropped on all fours, and swung herself over the staircase. Dave grabbed her.

"Come on, Tom!" he said, and the three of them ran frantically towards the fence and scrambled through, just as Mr. Sandman turned and, with the Engineer finally routed, returned unhesitatingly to his office.

Up in their hiding-place, Alice unfolded the plan, and Dave and Tommy bent over it with her.

"Oh," said Alice, "I nearly forgot."

She produced the distinctly crummy rock-cakes out of her pinafore pockets, and shared them impartially among the three of them.

"Look here," said Dave. "This shaft. It's marked *disused.*"

"Then we could use it to bring up the ponies!" said Alice.

"Eh, not too fast!" said Dave. "It depends how old it is, and how deep. Sometimes these old shafts only had a ladder down the side."

"Then we could climb down," said Alice, encouraged.

Dave looked at her.

"Aye, but the ponies couldn't climb up, could they? They're not much on ladders, are ponies."

"Oh," said Alice, her spirits somewhat dashed.

Girls didn't know much, thought Dave, tolerantly.

Alice picked up the plan, and jumped to her feet.

"Well," she said, "the first thing to do is to find it. Come on!"

She set off. Dave opened his mouth, and shut it again. What could he say? She was right. He scrambled to his feet and followed her, with Tommy scampering after them.

Until they climbed the slope and emerged on to the wide expanse of bramble and heather, Alice hadn't realized how very large the moors were. They were not flat, but were composed of little hills and hollows—and any one of the hollows could contain the shaft which they were looking for. Tommy was already dragging his short legs and heaving great sighs, and Dave and Alice gazed at each other in despair.

"Let's have another look at the plan," said Dave. "Here's where the Emsdale workings end."

"But we can't tell where that is," said Alice, "because it's underneath the ground."

"Aye, but see where it says 'Napp's Hill.' That's where we're standing now."

"Then the shaft shouldn't be far away."

They stared round them.

"I would have thought we would see it from here," said Dave, gloomily. "It's getting late. We'd best turn back."

"Oh no, we *can't!*" cried Alice. "Dave, we've got to find it. We must. Because if we don't find it soon, then all the machinery will be in, and then—"

She didn't finish, and Dave didn't want her to.

"All right," he said. "We'll just climb that next rise."

But the next rise only led on to another limitless and featureless expanse of moorland.

"I want me tea," said Tommy.

Alice and Dave both turned on him.

"You *would!*" said Dave, and Alice said, "Tommy, don't you *care* about the ponies?"

Tommy was shaken for a moment by the double attack, but then he fought back.

"I want me tea," he said again, "and I'm going home!"

He turned and went trudging off along the ridge. Dave and Alice looked at each other.

"He's not even going in the right direction," said Dave. "Eh, yer daft ha'porth!" he yelled. "Go on that way, and you'll fetch up in Leeds!"

Alice shivered. There was a cold wind now, and the sun was getting low in the sky.

"I suppose we'd better turn back," she said.

"Aye," said Dave. "It's hopeless. I don't reckon we'll ever find it."

They turned and began to walk back the way they had come.

"I don't really know what it looks like," Alice confessed.

"That's just the trouble," said Dave. "It could just be a hole in the ground, with a few planks over it."

"We'll never find *that!*" said Alice.

Dave sighed.

"I know," he said. He turned to look at the small, obstinate figure, trudging away in the wrong direction. "Tommy!" he yelled. "Will you come back here!"

The little figure trudged exasperatingly on.

"Oh no!" said Dave, recognizing one of Tommy's rare obstinate fits which could be ended by nothing but superior physical force. "I'll have to go and fetch him. You stay here."

"I'll come with you," said Alice.

The moors suddenly seemed very large and lonely.

"All right. Come on," said Dave.

It was infuriating to have to walk on and on in the wrong direction, knowing that they would only have to retrace their steps.

"I'll give him such a thumping when I reach him!" said Dave, his eyes fixed on the small figure on the skyline.

The small figure suddenly began to jump about, as though it had been stung by a wasp.

"He's gone mad," said Dave, resignedly.

But Tommy was shouting something as he jumped about, waving his arms and legs.

"I've found it, Dave! I've found it!"

Dave and Alice looked at each other and, with one accord, began to run.

It was in a little hollow, which was why they hadn't seen it from the top of the rise. There was a small head-stock—a miniature version of the big Emsdale winding wheels—and beside it a little brick building, half overgrown with bushes.

"That's the old engine-house," said Dave.

Behind the sagging wooden door, the engine was still there, covered with dust.

"Aye," said Dave. "It's a winding engine." And, in response to a look from Alice, "For winding the cage up and down."

They went outside again. The shaft was covered with rotting boards, but the wires still ran from the headstock to the engine-house.

"Then if we can get it working," said Alice, "we could bring the ponies up."

Dave looked from the shaft to the engine-house, and back at Alice's huge, shining eyes.

"Aye," he said. "We could."

CHAPTER TEN

THAT evening, Mr. Sandman sat in the drawing-room, reading his paper. He seemed to be quite engrossed in it, and rustled the pages a great deal as he turned them, but he was uneasily aware of Alice, reading a book at the table nearby. She had not spoken to him since their disastrous meeting in the office that morning, and he longed to apologize to her, but could not bring himself to do it. After all, he really had not been in the wrong, and what, if she asked him again, could he say about the ponies?

By the fireplace, empty except for the pampas grass which she had tenderly brought from London, sat Mrs. Sandman, knitting, and beside her Miss Coutts crocheted with a fierce determination which was all the more remarkable since all she was making was a white mat, just like dozens of other white mats in the workbag at her side.

"Father," said Alice, lowering her book, which bore the title, *Science for the Young,* "how does a winding engine work?"

Sandman readily put down his paper, only too glad that she was speaking to him again.

"Now, Alice, dear," said Miss Coutts, still crocheting rapidly on, "that is hardly a suitable subject for a young lady."

Sandman glanced between Alice's mutinous face and Miss Coutts' supremely smug assurance, and made up his mind.

"Miss Coutts," he said, "I want my daughter to be a

young lady. I want her to learn sewing, and French, and watercolors. But I also want her to take an interest in the things about her."

Mrs. Sandman glanced nervously at Miss Coutts. Would the Governess—who, Mrs. Sandman had learned, was distantly related to the Duke of Hertfordshire—think that was vulgar? Impossible to tell. Miss Coutts merely inclined her head in a stately manner, and continued to crochet.

"So, Alice," said Mr. Sandman, standing up, "if you'd like to come to my study, I will show you how a winding engine works."

Alice gave him a dazzling smile.

"Thank you, Father," she said.

In the old engine-house, Dave was trying to force two pieces of the machine together, after taking them apart to clean them.

"That piece should go there," said Alice, consulting first *Science for the Young* and then a pamphlet called *Mining Engineering*.

"No, it shouldn't," said Dave.

He struggled on.

"You're doing it all wrong," said Alice.

"No, I'm not. What do girls knows about engines? You can't get it in *there*. Any fool can see that!"

"You could, if you took that piece off," said Alice.

"No, you couldn't!" said Dave. "Here, I'll show you."

He tried it. It fitted perfectly. Dave glanced at Alice, who hastily bent over the diagram, without the faintest sign of a smile.

"Um . . ." said Dave.

Alice looked up.

"Where does this piece go?"

"Oh." Alice consulted the notes. "There. And then the nut goes through there."

Dave followed her instructions, and Tommy, standing by with a huge spanner, energetically turned the nut, at mortal peril to himself and everyone else. Dave looked at Alice with a smile, and she smiled happily back.

When it was all cleaned and put together again and tightened up, Dave stood back and looked at it.

"Now," he said, "it all needs greasing."

"Yes," Alice agreed, "but where can we get the oil?"

"Harry's got plenty," said Tommy.

"Who's Harry?" asked Alice.

Tommy was surprised to find that Dave was regarding him with unfeigned approval.

"Harry looks after the engine-house at Emsdale," said Dave.

The colliery engine-house was like the engine-room of a ship, but the great oily shaft pounding to and fro, instead of driving a screw, turned a huge, shiny spool of wire.

Harry, the engine-man, wiping his hands on a piece of oily rag, looked up to see Tommy standing in front of him.

"Hullo, Tommy," he said. "What do you want?"

"It's a big engine, Harry, isn't it?" said Tommy.

Harry was slightly surprised, because Dave and Tommy had been in and out of the engine-house almost since they learned to walk, but he replied,

"Aye, it's a big engine. It's got a lot to do."

He began to turn away.

"Harry!" said Tommy, quickly.

He had seen Dave darting round the back of the engine. Harry turned back.

"Aye?"

Tommy couldn't think of anything to say. He finally came up with,

"What does it have to do?"

"You know what it does!" said Harry. "Winds the cage up and down, and pumps the water out."

"Where does the water come from?" inquired Tommy.

A quick flick of his eyes showed him that Dave had found a tin of grease and was heading back for the doorway.

"*I* don't know where the water comes from," said Harry. "Everywhere, I suppose."

He began to turn away again. Tommy saw with alarm that Dave had returned for an oil-can which he had just spotted immediately behind Harry's back. The thundering noise of the engine covered his footsteps, but in another moment, Harry would . . . Fortunately, Harry thought of a further piece of instruction which he could bestow.

"If you didn't pump the pit out every day," he said,

leaning over the pressure gauge to emphasize his point, "it'd soon be flooded."

Tommy nodded and smiled. He couldn't think of anything more to ask. Harry prepared to turn away again. Dave was only halfway to the door with the grease and the oil-can.

"Harry!" cried Tommy.

Harry paused, and looked at him inquiringly. Another quick flick of the eyes showed Tommy that Dave had reached the door and was gone. Tommy gave Harry a dazzling, tooth-gapped smile.

"Good-bye, Harry," he said, and trotted out.

Harry looked after him, puzzled. Because he had kept his eyes on him throughout their conversation, he never did connect Tommy with the missing oil-can and tin of grease.

Stoking the engine at the old shaft proved to be unexpectedly hard work. Although it was much smaller than the main colliery engine, it seemed to have a voracious appetite, and the rusty old shovels which they had found in the grass behind the engine-house were dreadfully heavy. Alice and Tommy could only just lift them, and hardly managed to toss more than three or four lumps of coal into the fire at a time. Then, although they had been lucky to find a mound of coal behind the engine-house, abandoned with the profligacy customary in coal-mining districts, they had to trundle it round in an old iron wheelbarrow which was so heavy that they could hardly move it empty, let alone full of coal. They toiled on, however, until at last the pressure gauge showed that they had succeeded in getting up steam.

"Now," said Dave. "Let's see if we can bring the cage up."

He went to the controls. He felt like the captain of a ship on its maiden voyage. Alice and Tommy watched with triumphant smiles on their sooty faces. Dave pulled the lever into position, and turned the valve. The big spool of wire began to move. They all three beamed with joy. The wire stopped moving. The engine died.

"What is it?" cried Alice. "What's the matter with it?"

"I don't know," said Dave.

He banged the lever into position again.

"It must work, it *must!*"

"Turn the valve the other way," suggested Alice.

Dave did so. Nothing happened. They looked at each other helplessly. All that hard work—and to be so close to success—and now!

"There must be *something* we can do!" cried Alice.

A voice spoke behind them.

"What's going on here, then?"

They all jumped, caught their breath and turned. They saw Bert, his bait-box under his arm, eyeing them from the doorway. He was on his way to the pit after visiting his snares.

Dave jumped down from the platform.

"Oh—Bert," he said. "We were just—playing around."

"Trying to get the old engine to go, are you?"

"We-ell . . ."

Bert grinned.

"What are you going to do with it when you've got it going?"

"We're going to get the ponies up!" cried Tommy.

Alice poked him, and Dave glared at him. Bert chuckled.

"Oh, aye? And how do you think you're going to get them out?"

"Through the old workings," said Tommy, undaunted.

"Oh, Tommy!" cried Dave, despairingly.

Bert still looked amused. He turned to Dave.

"You're going to get the ponies up out of the pit—you and Tommy and the little Miss?"

Dave looked back at him defiantly.

"Yes. We are. Because otherwise they'll be sent to the slaughter-house."

"Aye," said Bert. He glanced at Alice, saw her face and looked quickly away again.

"But we won't let it happen," said Dave. "We're going to save them. Only we can't get the engine to—"

And then an awful thing happened. Dave's voice broke, just as if he were a little boy, and tears came into his eyes. Bert didn't seem to notice. He walked round the engine, peering at it.

"Shouldn't be too difficult," he said. "It's not *so* long since it was running."

Bert didn't seem to do much. A general tightening of nuts and screws. A round piece of metal taken off, turned upside-down and replaced. The lever slammed more securely home, and a little iron bar jammed in an eyelet and secured.

"Now then," he said, and returned to the steam-valve.

Slowly the driving shaft of the engine came to life, rose and fell, drove forward and back and rose again. Slowly but steadily the big spool of wire began to turn. Dave remained where he was, carefully watching Bert so as to be sure that he knew how to work it himself, but Alice and Tommy ran outside. They saw the black wheel turning above the shaft and heard a rumble from below, and then at last the cage rose into sight from its prison and came to rest. It was much smaller and simpler than the cage at Emsdale—merely an open wooden box, with a single iron bar to secure its occupants. But it was quite big enough to take a pony.

Alice and Tommy hugged each other and danced about and then Alice did a cartwheel in a swirl of frilly petticoat and knickers, and Tommy endeavored to do a handstand, with the seat of his trousers much higher than his boots. Bert came out of the engine-house with Dave and grinned his toothless grin.

"I should run it up and down a few times," he said, "to work the grease in."

Dave nodded.

"But don't run it too long," Bert added, "or someone might hear it."

He looked at Alice and Tommy, all grimy and beaming.

"Thank you, Bert!" cried Alice. "Oh, thank you!"

Bert pretended to scowl.

"Don't thank *me*," he said. "There's no sense in any of it." He began to move off. "I must get to the stables, or I'll lose me money."

"You won't tell Luke, Bert, will you?" Dave demanded urgently.

Bert stopped and looked at him.

"Me?" he said. "I'm not telling anyone!" He looked at them each in turn. "Now, mind," he said, "I've never seen you here, and I don't know what you're doing."

"No, Bert," said Dave, obediently, and Bert couldn't resist a little smile as he turned and plodded away in the direction of Emsdale.

It was getting late when Dave, Alice and Tommy

climbed out of the hollow and looked back at the wheel and engine-house below.

"I'll go down tomorrow," said Dave, "and try to find a way through to the present workings."

"And the stables," said Tommy.

"Aye," said Dave.

"Will it be safe to go down there?" asked Alice.

" 'Course it will!" Dave replied, over-emphatically because he knew that it wasn't.

"You ought to take a canary down," said Alice, "to make sure there isn't any gas."

She knew from *Science for the Young,* as well as from listening to her father, that if there was any question of bad air, a canary was always taken down to give the first warning of danger.

"Aye, well," said Dave, with a grin, "we haven't got a canary, so I'll just have to take a chance instead."

They began to walk on towards the village.

"If you go down alone," said Tommy, after thinking it over, "you'll get lost."

"No, I won't," said Dave.

"Yes, you will. You don't know the old workings, and there won't be any light."

"I'll take a candle."

"You'll get lost," Tommy repeated, obstinately.

"Oh, give over!" said Dave, crossly.

Alice looked troubled.

"You won't go down till I come?"

"Won't be able to," said Dave. "I'll need you and Tommy to stoke the engine and take the cage up and down. Are you sure you can get away?"

"Oh yes," said Alice, confidently. "That's no trouble!"

Alice had made two useful discoveries about Miss Coutts. As a matter of fact, she had made several more, but these were the most valuable. First, Miss Coutts hated going out of the house, because there was always a wind blowing off the moors, and it made her hair untidy. Secondly, she had a secret taste for romantic novels. There was nothing she liked better than putting on her rimless glasses on their gold chain, and settling down in the basket chair in the schoolroom, with a book called *The Golden Wine of Youth,* by Mrs. Belmont, or *Little*

Sunshine, by Lancelot Cavendish. So that, although she often suggested taking Alice for a walk in the afternoon, almost any excuse was enough to convince her that there was no need for her to venture out, and that Alice could safely amuse herself until supper-time.

"Miss Coutts," said Alice, as they finished lunch the next day, "I think I *would* like to learn to crochet, after all."

"Oh—yes, dear, of course," replied Miss Coutts. She was delighted that Alice was at last showing one ladylike inclination, especially since only the day before she had said that she hated needlework, and that she thought she would hate crochet even more. On the other hand— Miss Coutts made up her mind to do her duty. "I will teach you this afternoon," she said.

"Thank you, Miss Coutts," said Alice, and Mrs. Sandman heaved a sigh of relief.

Perhaps, after all, it was worth putting up with the Governess's chilly superiority and disapproval if she could really succeed in turning Alice into a young lady.

Up in the schoolroom, Miss Coutts produced a large spool of thread from her workbag, and a brand-new shiny crochet-hook.

"Now, dear," she said, "you make a loop, and then—"

Alice gave the lesson her full attention, and had soon mastered the basic stitch, so that she could take from Miss Coutts the crochet-hook and spool of thread, and start to turn the loop into an ever-growing lacy circle. Miss Coutts, seeing her engrossed, surreptitiously took up her novel. Would Little Sunshine reform her disagreeable curmudgeon of a Guardian? Would Sir Harry realize in time that she was not really a child, but a young girl, hungry for the love she had never had?

Alice rose to her feet.

"I think I've got it now," she announced. "I'll just go and practice."

"Alice!" cried Miss Coutts.

But Alice had gone.

Miss Coutts heard the back door bang down below, and, surprised, went to the window. She watched Alice running through the garden, and scrambling up the hill. She really ought to go after her. On the other hand— The call of Little Sunshine proved too strong. Miss Coutts sat down by the fire. "Oh, Guardian, dear Guardian, do not send me away!" Miss Coutts wiped away a tear.

"Here you are," said Alice, giving Dave the spool of thread. "Tie one end to a post at the bottom of the shaft, and unroll it as you go. Then you can find your way back."

"Nay," said Dave, smiling. "I don't need—"

"Take it!" Alice commanded, "or I won't help Tommy work the engine, and then you can't go down!"

Dave shook his head, but took the thread and put it in his pocket. He stuck a candle in a ball of clay, and put matches in his other pocket and stepped into the cage.

"Promise you'll keep hold of the thread," said Alice.

"All right," he answered.

Alice lowered the bar, and then she and Tommy returned to the engine-house. Dave took hold of the upright of the cage. He hoped Alice didn't know what an awful risk he was taking, or how frightened he was.

"Help me," said Alice, struggling with the lever. "I can't get it to—Tommy, help me."

Tommy climbed on to the platform with her, and together they wrestled it into place, and put the bolt into its slot. Alice turned towards the valve, looked at Tommy and swallowed. She took a deep breath and turned it.

Dave held tightly to the upright as the cage began to descend. The darkness came to meet him, and slowly intensified. The wind rushed past him.

In the engine-house, Alice kept her eyes fixed on the little piece of wood on a wire, descending the short distance between one white paint mark and another. Supposing she did it wrong! Supposing the cage, with Dave in it, crashed straight to the bottom of the shaft! Frantically she began to turn the valve back.

"It's not there yet," said Tommy.

"Yes, it is."

But she eased the valve, and then turned it again and the piece of wood came to rest by the white paint mark.

The cage reached the bottom and stopped with a slight jar. It was so dark that Dave felt as though he was shut up in a box. Often as he had been below ground, he still had to fight down his panic as he felt for the matches. The tiny light flared. For a moment the candle wouldn't light. It seemed an hour before at last the wick caught, and flickered, and burned steadily. Dave took a deep breath, and stepped out of the cage. He held up the candle and saw a passage ahead of him, and prepared to set out. The heavy spool of thread thumping about in his jacket pocket reminded him, and he took it out, and hesitated. He almost didn't bother, but then he thought of his promise to Alice, and, with a tolerant smile for female whims, he put the candle down, in its ball of clay, tied the thread round a convenient pit prop, picked the candle up and set out again, unrolling the thread as he went.

Above the shaft, Alice and Tommy sat clasping their knees in the bright sunshine. A curlew called shrilly from the moors beyond.

"My dad died down the pit," said Tommy.

Alice looked at him, startled.

"He did? Was it—an explosion? I've heard my father talk about fire-damp. That's a sort of gas, isn't it?"

"Aye," said Tommy. "It builds up, and you get a spark and it goes up." He added, with gloomy relish, "You never know when it'll happen."

Alice looked, dismayed, down the black shaft.

The candle flickered in Dave's hand, and he stood still. In spite of what he had said to Alice, he wished that he *did* have a canary to give him warning of carbon monoxide. He remembered his father saying that canaries were affected by this deadly gas even more swiftly than men were, and that when the bird fell unconscious in its cage, this was the time for miners to retreat hastily into fresher air, where they survived and the canary was soon revived. Without such warning, Dave knew that if the carbon monoxide was present, even in quite a small amount, he could be dead in a few moments. In his mind were all the stories he had heard of disasters in the pit— of explosions set off by a naked flame, or even a spark, of the deaths and injuries and of the deadly after-damp which came upon those fleeing from the explosion, so that men and boys were found lying calm and dead where they had fallen, before they even knew that it was there.

The old workings were very uneven, with unexpected twists and turns, sudden dips in the floor and changes of roof-height. The spool of thread unrolling in Dave's hand was, after all, a great comfort to him. He had hoped at first that he would be able to keep some sense

of direction and make his way towards the present workings, but he soon knew that he had no idea whether he
was walking towards the present workings or away from
them. He thought of turning back and trying one of the
dozens of other passages which led off on either side, but
what would be the use? He knew that he could blunder
about for hours and never find his way through.

Dave turned a corner. The dim light of the candle,
barely pushing the darkness a few feet away from him,
struck upon upright planks of wood. Dave held the candle
higher. The passage was blocked off with timbers. Dave's
shoulders drooped. He prepared to turn back. And then,
from beyond the timbers, he heard voices and the rattle
of iron on iron. He lowered the candle, but light still
came through the chinks. Hardly able to believe it, Dave
moved towards the barrier and peered through. The
rattling sound drew nearer, and suddenly, right before his
eyes, there was Flash, trundling along at his usual ener-
getic pace, with Ginger panting behind. As he drew
level, Flash slackened speed, turned his head and stopped.
Ginger, who had been stealing a ride on the tongue of
the wagon, fell off and swore.

"Flash!" he yelled. "What's the matter with you? Get
on, will yuh?"

Flash, feeling the reins slapping on his back, shook
his head and trotted on. Dave, his face enraptured, turned
and began to hurry back the way he had come. He left
the spool of thread lying beneath the timbers, where he
had put it as he peered through.

Alice and Tommy leaned on their shovels by the winding-engine.

"How far will he have to go?" asked Alice, "to get
through to the present workings?"

"Hard to say," replied Tommy, knowledgeably. "Them
levels run for miles. Most likely he'll get lost."

"Tommy!" cried Alice. "He won't!"

"His candle will burn out," said Tommy, with ghoulish
relish, "and he'll wander about in the darkness until he
falls exhausted and lies there, clemmed to death, nothing
left but a skelington!"

Alice dropped her shovel, took hold of him and shook
him until his teeth rattled in his head.

"He won't!" she shouted. "Be quiet! He won't!"

A hiss of steam drew Alice's attention, and she released Tommy and seized the shovel again.

"Pressure's dropping!" she cried. "Come on!"

She began to stoke furiously, and Tommy, mildly surprised at her vehemence, came to help her.

Down in the old workings, Dave came to a place where two passages led off in different directions. He paused, and felt for the thread. He could not find it. He made his mind up and turned into the nearest passage, followed it along by the dim light of the candle and found to his dismay that the roof was getting lower and lower. He knew what it was—a "creeping," where the roof and the floor moved together, until there was barely room to crawl. He knew that he had not traveled along that passage earlier. He retraced his steps, and took the other passage and then came to a choice of two other levels. He had no idea which to take. He was lost. Reaching forward with his foot, he found that he was stepping on nothing. He drew back. He was on the edge of an abyss.

Alice came out of the engine-house and looked about her. Tommy had lost interest in the stoking, and was practicing handstands a little distance away.

"Tommy!" she called. "Come and help me wind the cage up. I'm going down."

Tommy scrambled to his feet.

"You can't!"

"Yes, I can," said Alice. "I'm sure he's lost. I'm going to go and look for him. You can wind me down, and then go for help."

"Then we'll have to tell everyone what we're doing. They won't let us get the ponies."

Alice hesitated.

"Yes. All right. You stay here, and I'll go down."

"You'll get lost as well!" said Tommy.

"No, I won't," replied Alice, stoutly. She threw a glance towards the shaft. It looked terrifyingly black and deep. "Come and help me to stoke the engine, and then you can wind me down."

Dave, standing on the edge of the abyss, waited until he had got his courage back, and then stooped down and felt in front of him. The ground did fall steeply away, but only for a foot or so, and then curved up again. He had merely struck an unevenness in the surface. He tilted the candle down, and saw by its light a pale line along the blackness of the floor. He reached out for it, and found it was Alice's crochet thread. He drew a great breath of relief—which in itself was a help, because he had been running short of oxygen merely by holding his breath in fear!—and straightened up. With the thread in one hand and the candle in the other, he began to step out with confidence. Even if he was walking in the wrong direction, he would arrive at the barrier and then could simply turn and follow the thread back. But, in fact, his sense of direction had not failed him. The thread brought him straight back to the bottom of the shaft.

"You're not really going down, are you?" asked Tommy, as Alice flung a final shovel-full of coal in the furnace and closed the door.

"Yes, I am," said Alice. "He might not have got lost. He might have had an accident, or been overcome by gas or—"

"Then you will be, too," said Tommy, with his usual logic. "Anyway, I can't work the engine. I don't know how to."

"I'll show you," said Alice.

They went into the engine-house—and at that moment the signal-bell rang above their heads.

"It's Dave!" cried Alice, and, both beaming with relief, she and Tommy raced towards the controls.

By the time Dave reached the surface, he had got over his fright and was feeling very pleased with himself. Alice and Tommy hurried out of the engine-house to meet him.

"Dave!" called Alice. "Did you get through? What did you find?"

"Did you get lost, Dave?" asked Tommy.

" 'Course not!" said Dave, and then, with a touch of guilty haste at the lie, "We can get right through to the coal-face, where they're working now. I saw Flash."

"Flash!" cried Alice, and she and Tommy clutched each other joyfully.

"There's only timbers blocking it off," said Dave, "so when the time comes, we can break through, bring them back that way and then close it up again. No one will ever know we've been there."

A sense of mischief suddenly overcame them all, and they laughed and giggled until Tommy rolled on the ground—something he was never averse to doing.

"They'll look for the ponies, and they won't be there!"

cried Alice, gleefully. "And all the time, we'll have them and we'll keep them safe for . . ."

An awful thought struck her. She stopped short, her face full of horror. Tommy sat up, surprised.

"What is it?" said Dave, alarmed.

"Where are we going to keep them?"

"Oh, is *that* all?" said Dave. "Don't worry about that. I know the very place. It's on the way home. Come on. We'll shut the engine down, and then I'll show you."

CHAPTER ELEVEN

"SORRY I'm late, Mum," said Clara, bringing tea into the drawing-room. "I thought Miss Alice might be back."

"Back? Where is she?" asked Mrs. Sandman, startled.

"She went out after lunch," replied Clara. "Over the moors."

"Oh. With Miss Coutts."

"Huh!" said Clara. "Not much, she didn't!"

She went to fetch the cake-stand and plonked it down beside Mrs. Sandman. Mrs. Sandman watched her with some apprehension.

"Miss Alice went out alone," said Clara.

"Then where is Miss Coutts?"

"Sitting upstairs, with her feet on the fender, reading that book of hers!" said Clara, and went out, with the satisfied expression of one who has paid off several scores in a highly public-spirited manner.

Up in the schoolroom, Miss Coutts had reached the last chapter of her book. Esmé, better known as Little Sunshine, was lying ill of a brain-fever. Sir Harry had at last realized that she loved him, and was galloping to her side, furiously whipping his horse, which was not like him, for beneath his stern exterior, he was a gentle and tender-hearted man. Would he arrive in time to give Little Sunshine the will to live? Miss Coutts turned a page eagerly.

"Miss Coutts!" said Mrs. Sandman from the doorway. "Where is Alice?"

"Oh," said Miss Coutts. Nothing could have been further from her thoughts at that moment than Alice. She hastily slid the book down on to the chair and stood up.

"Clara said she went out on the moors—*alone*," said Mrs. Sandman.

Miss Coutts quickly struck back.

"I'm afraid Alice has been allowed altogether too much liberty," she said. "I was teaching her crochet after lunch, and then she left the room and—quite without permission, went out for a walk."

"But where is she *now?*" demanded Mrs. Sandman.

Miss Coutts threw a quick glance at the clock on the mantelpiece. It certainly was a great deal later than she had thought.

"I will go and find her," she said. "She can't be far away."

Mrs. Sandman stood back to let her pass. Miss Coutts, feeling that she had, for once, allowed Mrs. Sandman to win that particular skirmish, decided to recapture her lost ground. She paused, and shook her head reprovingly at Mrs. Sandman.

"We really must try," she said, "to teach Alice the meaning of discipline."

To Alice, dancing through the heather, it was as though the ponies were already rescued and her dream had come true.

"Come, Flash!" she cried, tugging on an imaginary bridle. "Come, Bluey, Lion, Soldier!"

And Dave and Tommy got caught up in it, too.

"Flash! Bluey! Sandy, True, Jester! Come, Star!"

They were surrounded by the pit ponies, prancing on printless hooves and tossing their heads in the sunshine.

"This way," said Dave, turning aside on to a faint track which led off at right-angles from the main path.

They climbed a small rise, and saw a square gray chimney ahead.

"Is it another mine?" asked Alice.

"Aye," Dave answered, "a lead mine."

It was like a large barn, half-hidden in a fold of rough ground. Dave pushed open the broken-down door, and they crept inside. There was only a dim light, from a glassless window high up in the wall, and the stone floor was strewn with straw.

"Doesn't anyone come here?"

"Nay," answered Dave, "not since the lead mine closed down, and that was years ago. Sometimes in the winter, the shepherd'll bring the sheep in, but no one comes near it in the summer time."

They wandered about, and looked at each other with shining eyes.

"No one would ever think of looking here," said Alice. "It's hidden from the path—"

"And the window's too high to look in," said Tommy.

"We can bring them here and keep them safe forever and ever," said Alice.

Dave thought it time to bring them all down to earth.

"We'll need fodder," he said. "There's plenty in the barn behind the engine-house at Emsdale. We'll have to fetch it out, bit by bit, and hide it, and then bring it up here. They're heavy, mind, those bales. Most like, we'll have to bring them up one at a time."

Tommy sighed. Rescuing ponies was turning out to be very hard work indeed.

"How long do you think we've got?" asked Alice.

Dave shook his head.

"Don't know. Bert says they're going to use the ponies to haul the machinery and cables and that, so we're all right until it's all installed, but I don't know how long that'll be."

He and Alice looked at each other soberly. The responsibility of their task fell upon them again, more heavily because of their recent light-heartedness.

"Never mind," said Alice, encouragingly. "We know we can get them out, and we know where we're going to bring them. That's the main thing."

"Aye," said Dave, cheered.

Tommy ran outside, and Dave and Alice followed more slowly.

"We must be sure always to shut the door," said Dave, "and make it look as though no one comes here."

He struggled to drag the sagging planks across the flag-stone, and Alice helped him to lift the rusty latch into its socket. They stood still for a moment, and Alice said, "Dave, I'm sorry about your father."

Dave looked at her, startled, and then away.

At first Alice thought she had offended him. Then he said in a low voice.

"Bert says the pit belongs to him, and to all them that died there."

He looked up at her. Alice nodded. They stood in silence, while a chaffinch piped in the trees behind the mine and goldfinches flashed in the thistles and their friendship took possession of a new and valuable territory which it would never lose.

They climbed the uneven ground behind the chimney. Tommy was hopping on one foot on the top of the rise. As Dave and Alice turned towards the path which led to the village, they heard a shrill voice in the distance.

"Alice! Alice!"

Startled, they saw a black figure gesticulating.

"Miss Coutts!" cried Alice. "Quick, run!"

Dave grabbed Tommy and they took to their heels in the opposite direction. Alice hurried towards Miss Coutts, anxious that she should not see the lead mine, and Miss Coutts came to meet her. She wore her hat, with a gray scarf wound round it to keep it on, but she still held it with one hand and held her skirts up with the other, and she looked about her nervously, as though she was ven-turing into Indian country.

"Alice!" she called, as soon as she got near. "Where have you been?"

"Oh—just out on the moors."

"But, who was that I saw with you? It looked like—*boys!*"

"Yes," said Alice. She saw the horror in Miss Coutts' face. A flash of inspiration came to her. "Their father owns the mine."

"Oh," said Miss Coutts. *"Really?"* She was about to turn and look after the fleeing figures, but a gust of wind caught the edge of her hat, and she had to clutch it, and tighten the scarf. "You must invite them home to tea, dear," she said.

Alice hadn't thought of that. She hesitated.

"They—er—I don't think they'd come."

She and her governess had begun to walk back towards the house. Miss Coutts paused, looking earnestly down at her.

"You mean, because their father is a colliery owner, and your father only manages the mine? Alice, dear, you must remember that to the true aristocrat, all men are equal."

Alice glanced over her shoulder. Two ragamuffin figures in clumsy clothes and heavy boots pranced happily along on the skyline.

"Yes, Miss Coutts," said Alice.

CHAPTER TWELVE

"Eh, you, Flash!" shouted Luke. "What do you think you're doing with my bait-box?"

Crouched, naked to the waist, in a four-foot-high stall at the coal-face, he saw Flash nibbling at the square tin which hung with his coat in the narrow roadway. Luke crawled out.

"Do you think there's something in there for you?" he demanded. "Geroff!"

Despite his angry tone, Flash continued to nuzzle confidently at the bait-box.

"Come on, then!" said Luke.

He took the tin down, pushing Flash's nose aside, and opened it. Flash nudged him, and Luke grinned, and gave him a crust of bread and jam. He watched, his teeth white in his black face, as the pony took it with gentle lips and chomped it past the coarse iron bit. Luke closed the tin and put it back on its nail.

"Go on," he said. "Get off with you."

He crawled back into the stall, but didn't set to work again at once. He watched as Ginger turned Flash round and attached the full tubs to the limber-frame, and his mates, Amos and Big Alf, who shoveled the coal which he dug, watched, too. They saw the small head, patient under the clumsy leather and iron bridle, the neat hooves and the powerful hind-quarters, like a miniature cart-horse. Then Ginger had slammed the iron bolt home, and, without waiting for a command, Flash set off with the full tubs of coal, little legs going like pistons, and vanished into the darkness.

Luke, Amos and Alf glanced at each other, and then Luke set furiously to work. There was a shower of stones from the roof, and his safety lamp flared. Alf and Amos looked at each other quickly. Luke paused, and then worked on, his muscles straining in the narrow space. Another, heavier fall of dust and stones made him pause again.

"Luke!" cried Amos. "Will you come out from there!"

"Nay, it's well enough," said Luke, preparing to wield his pickaxe again.

"Come on, Luke," said Alf. "It's as like to come down on us as it is on thee!"

Luke grinned, and crawled out.

"Fetch in some more timbers," he said, "and we'll shore it up."

It seemed a long shift that day, and Luke thought how much longer it would seem with only the iron rattle of machinery instead of the brave clatter of small hooves and the nuzzling of a soft, greedy mouth to break the long monotony of darkness, dust and sweat.

"Sorry, lads," said Sam Carter, as they crossed the yard on their way home, "there'll be no work for you tomorrow."

They turned towards him.

"There'll be no coal-getting while the machinery is connected up."

"And how long will that take?" Alf demanded.

Sam Carter shrugged.

"Not more than a day or two. Manager's in Sheffield, trying to find some new buyers. When he's back, and the machinery's been tested, then you'll be able to work again."

The miners glanced at each other, and moved off. Luke lingered.

"How long till the ponies are gone?"

"They'll do their last haulage tomorrow, and be brought up next day."

Luke nodded. He and Sam looked at each other in silence for a moment, before Luke followed his mates towards the gate.

"Will you be home for your dinner?" asked Violet next morning.

"Nay," said Luke, "I'll not hang about the house all day. Give me my bait-box as usual. I'll take Pearl up on the moors—see if we can get a rabbit."

He glanced at Dave, and Dave knew that Luke was wondering whether to suggest that the boys should come, too. Dave bent his head over his porridge, and Tommy, after a quick look at Dave, did the same.

The boys were still at breakfast when Luke went to the door, and whistled Pearl. Violet brought him his lunchbox.

"Thanks, love," he said, and Dave, glancing up, was startled by the way his mother smiled.

Luke opened the door, and paused. He stood still for a moment and then turned back.

"Dave!" he said.

He said it very harshly, and the word seemed to come out with a great effort. Dave was instantly alert and hostile, and, under his cold stare, Luke seemed to have some trouble in continuing. He glanced at Violet, and then back at Dave.

"They're connecting up the machinery today," he said, "and tomorrow the ponies will be brought up and sent to Barnsley. This is their last day in the pit."

Dave stared back at him without speaking.

"If you want to go down and see them," said Luke, roughly, "I'll make it all right with Sam Carter."

Dave felt confused and angry. It was kind of Luke— very kind—but he didn't want Luke to be kind. And then he realized that Luke's offer endangered the rescue of the ponies, and it was easy to shrug and reply carelessly, "No, thanks. I'm not bothered."

Violet and Luke exchanged a glance.

"Don't you want to say good-bye to them, Dave?" said Violet. "Not even old Flash?"

"They're only ponies," said Dave, and buried his face in his coronation mug.

Down in the pit that evening the ponies were still hard at work. They were not harnessed with the limber-frames, but with trace gear, with chains which could be attached to sledges for hauling timber and machinery. Engineers were busy connecting the main-and-tail hauler, and Bert strolled up to watch.

"That's right, Ginger," called the Deputy, as Flash trotted by with his load. "Take that up to the drift heading."

"Poor beasts," said Bert, as Flash vanished into the dimly-lit main roadway, and another pony followed him. "They don't know they're hauling that to their death."

The Deputy glanced at him, but didn't answer at first. Then he said, "What will you do, Bert, after the ponies are gone?"

"I've not thought," Bert replied. His face changed, as the reality of the situation came home to him for the first time. "Nay," he said, "there's no place for me in Emsdale now. I'll have to trudge and look for a job."

The Deputy glanced up at the big engine.

"Some others, too, I shouldn't wonder," he said.

"Aye," said Bert.

He began to stroll back towards the stables, and then paused. He thought he heard, far away, the sound of an engine. Three pitmen, engaged in shifting timber, heard it, too.

"What's that? Them engineers haven't got their machines working up at the face, have they?" said one.

"Nay," said another, "it sounds like a winding engine. You heard it, Bert, didn't you?"

Bert didn't answer for a moment. Then he looked at them solemnly, each in turn.

"Aye," he said, "I heard it. A winding engine. I've heard it before."

They looked at each other, and at Bert.

"It comes from the old workings," said Bert. He dropped his voice. They leaned forward to listen. "That road's been blocked off since ten men were killed there in a fall."

"Aye, that's true," said one of the men.

They glanced in the direction of the distant thumping.

"I'd not go near there for a hundred pound," said Bert.

"I'd be afraid the hobgoblins would drag me down into the old workings."

One of the other men forced a laugh.

"You're an old woman, Bert!" he said. "Hobgoblins!"

The others smiled, too, but they were very uneasy smiles.

"Come on, lads," said the first man. "Time to be getting up now, anyway."

And they finished piling the timber in its place and began to move off towards the pit-bottom. Bert saw them throw hasty glances over their shoulders as they went, and he grinned to himself. Miners are as superstitious as sailors, but don't admit it. He knew they'd never mention the sound of the winding engine to anyone else, for fear of being laughed at.

Back from the moors, and having delivered two plump bunnies to Violet, Luke strolled up to the colliery, where Sam Carter was checking the maintenance men and engine wrights as they stepped out of the cage.

"Any work for my mate and me tomorrow?" asked Luke.

"Might be, Luke," replied Sam. "Manager gets back from Sheffield tonight, and the machinery's all in, and ready to be used."

Luke looked at him in silence for a moment, and then he asked quietly, "Are they bringing in machines to cut the coal, Sam?"

Sam hesitated.

"They may bring in a few, but it'll only be—"

"To put us out of work!"

"Nay, nay!" cried Sam. "They'll help to win more coal, and make the pit pay better. Be good for all of us."

He saw Luke's face, full of suspicion.

"The Manager says—"

"The Manager!" exclaimed Luke, disgustedly. "What does he know? A little, primping fellow, with his black suit and his gold watch and his shiny boots! He's never worked at the coal-face in his life!"

"Nay," said Sam, "but he's been to the University and taken a degree in engineering."

Luke laughed.

"Oh, aye? He should try using his degree when the fire-damp's high, and the roof's creeping, and he wonders if

his next blow will be his last! Come on, Sam, you think
no more of him than I do!"

Sam struggled with himself. He didn't like the Manager,
it was true.

"He's a knowing sort of chap, and he means to succeed."
He stopped short.

"Did you hear something?"

"Have they started the new engine, down below?" asked
Luke.

"Nay, it sounded more as if it came from over the hill."

They both listened, and heard the distant rumble of
thunder. Luke smiled one of his rare, reluctant smiles.

"Aye, well," he said, "I reckon it was only the storm.
One machine's enough, after all—too many, I shouldn't
wonder!"

At the old pit-head, Dave and Tommy were toiling away,
stoking the winding engine. Dave paused to look anxiously
at the pressure gauge.

"Hurry up, Tom!" he said. "Get some more coal!"

Tommy, struggling with the great iron wheelbarrow in
the failing light, scowled.

"Where's Alice?" he said.

Dave looked worried.

"She'll come as soon as she can get away."

"When'll that be?"

"How do I know?" said Dave, crossly.

"Supposing she doesn't come?" inquired Tommy, with
his usual exasperating habit of pursuing logic.

"She *must!*" said Dave, with a note of desperation. "It'll
take two of us to fetch the ponies out, and someone's
got to work the controls."

Tommy looked at the stormy red sky, and the fading
light.

"But if she doesn't come," he asked, "what will we do?"

Dave didn't answer. If Alice didn't come, the ponies
were doomed.

In Emsdale pit, Ginger unhitched the trace gear from
Flash's harness, and watched him turn and shake his head,
and trot with determination away in the direction of the
stable.

"That Flash!" he said. "He always knows when his shift
is over."

Another driver was unhitching Jester near by.

"It's over this time with a vengeance!" he said.

Ginger looked at him quickly, and then they both looked after Flash, as he disappeared into the darkness.

"Aye," said Ginger. "I reckon it is."

CHAPTER THIRTEEN

It had been a worrying day for Alice. She had thought of escaping after lunch, and not returning, but she was afraid that if she was still absent at supper-time, there might be a hue and cry, in which they would all be discovered. So then she decided to go to bed as usual, wait until her father had kissed her good night and then steal out of the house. The only trouble with that was that her father was in Sheffield, and no one seemed certain what time he would be returning. As the evening dragged on, she watched the fading light in the stormy sky, and listened to the rumble of the thunder, and thought of Dave and Tommy toiling away with shovel and wheelbarrow. She thought of the ponies, too.

"It's their last day," Dave had said, bobbing down behind the wall as Miss Coutts spied from the schoolroom window. "We've got to get them out tonight."

Alice suddenly made up her mind. She stretched and yawned.

"I'm awfully tired, Miss Coutts," she said. "I think I'll go to bed."

"Already, dear?" said Miss Coutts, startled.

"It was that geography," Alice explained. "Geography is very tiring."

It seemed a terrible waste to have a bath, but at least

Alice hoped it would give time for her father to arrive. She sat up in bed when she heard footsteps on the stairs, but then she heard her mother's voice.

"Miss Coutts," said Mrs. Sandman, surprised, "is Alice in bed already? She isn't ill, is she?"

"I don't think so," Miss Coutts replied. "She just seems to be very sleepy."

"Well—I'll just say good night to her," said Mrs. Sandman.

Alice hastily lay down again, and closed her eyes. The door opened, and she was aware of the light of the lamp as Mrs. Sandman tiptoed forward. She put the lamp down, and bent and kissed her.

"Good night, dear," she said.

Alice opened her eyes, and murmured drowsily, "Good night, Mother. Is Father home?"

"No, not yet, dear. I'm afraid he must be coming on the last train."

Alice closed her eyes again, and Mrs. Sandman picked up the lamp and went to the door. A sudden thought struck Alice, and she sat up quickly, but Mrs. Sandman had tiptoed out and shut the door. Alice sighed. She hadn't asked what time the last train arrived. She sat and thought, anxiously, and then made up her mind. She leaped out of bed and hastily began to dress.

Lightning was flashing now and then across the moors as Alice turned the bolster endways in her bed and carefully tucked the sheets over it. It certainly was rather fatter than she was, but she hoped that the hump it made in the bed would be enough to deceive anyone who only stood in the doorway holding up a lamp or candle. She put on her coat, pulled on her beret and opened the window. There was an apple-tree outside. She had never climbed down it yet, but there was one branch which was not too far away, and she hoped to be able to reach it. She also hoped that it was strong enough to bear her weight.

Alice sat on the window-sill and swung her legs out. All she had to do was to slide out until her feet reached the branch. But the branch was much further away than she had thought, and when at last she got her feet on to it, it sagged terrifyingly. She gripped the window-ledge for dear life, turned herself over and prepared to push away. As she did so, she looked down, and saw with dismay how far she would fall if she overbalanced. She took a deep breath, turned back again and reached up and grabbed hold of a branch above her head. Then she slid out again until her feet touched the bough, and, without giving herself time to think, swung herself out into space. The tree shook, and twigs crackled, and her booted feet slipped on the bough, but she managed to hang on until she had found a firmer footing in a fork of the main trunk. After that it was fairly easy to climb down. Delighted with her success, she jumped the last part, and landed on the edge of an old galvanized iron bath, which overturned with a clatter loud enough to be heard a mile away.

Horrified, Alice picked herself up and ran for the garden wall. She heard the kitchen door open behind her, and heard Clara's voice, sharpened with alarm.

"Who's there? Who is it?"

Alice tumbled over the stone wall and lay flat in the dewy grass. Had Clara seen her, or had she been dazzled by looking from the lighted kitchen into the nearly dark garden?

"Nobody there," said Clara. "Must've been that blessed cat!"

The door closed, and Alice scrambled to her feet and ran up the hill.

The end of the table in the Armstrong house was still laid with two places and two coronation mugs. Luke and Violet had finished their tea long since, and Luke sat with his pipe, pretending to read the paper while Violet darned socks. He looked towards the window.

"Did you hear something?"

Violet glanced up at him, but said nothing. Luke got up and went to the door. He opened it, and stood in the doorway. After a moment, Violet came to join him, her mending still in her hand.

"Listen," said Luke.

They heard a distant rumble.

"Thunder," said Violet.

"That's what Sam Carter said, but . . . it sounds more like—"

They both stood still, listening, and then heard a rumble much nearer, and the sound of a whistle as the train drew into the station. Luke looked down at Violet, and smiled, feeling foolish.

"The Sheffield train," she said, answering the smile.

"Aye, I know," he said, and they turned inside again, and shut the door.

Mr. Sandman was the only passenger to descend on to the deserted platform. He gave his ticket to the ticket collector, and, as the train pulled out again in a rush of steam, he went down the flight of steps which led towards the lane. He walked heavily, because he was tired. Somewhere at the back of his mind was satisfaction at what he had achieved, but arguing and bargaining did not come naturally to him, and the exercise of such powers gave him no pleasure. A man's work should be sufficient justification. He should not have to act as a huckster. He should not have to go like a traveling salesman round gray stone buildings, persuading well-fed, brusque Sheffield businessmen to buy his wares. But he had done it because he had responsibilities, and they must be fulfilled, no matter how.

Mr. Sandman glanced towards the village. There were no lights. The village street was unlit, and all the inhabitants were in bed. He thought of the miners, some of whom he now knew by name, and of the wives and children whom he had seen in the village, or walking up the lane. Perhaps it was true that all the hard work he had done during the past weeks had not been done *for them*, but at least it was because of what he had done that they would be fed and housed and clothed—and perhaps a great deal better in the future than they had been in the past.

Mr. Sandman felt, after all, a glow of pleasure behind his tiredness, and it was enhanced as he approached his own house, with the lighted window, as usual, welcoming him home. He had not lately come home with his customary enjoyment, because of the slight breach between himself and Alice. Perhaps it was partly due to the arrival of the Governess, which meant that he saw much less of his daughter, and that she was never in the hall now to kiss him and show her pleasure in his return. And he himself had been so busy that he had hardly seen her except at weekends, and then she always seemed to be in the custody of Miss Coutts. But still he did have an uneasy feeling that their relationship, behind all this, was not as warm as it had been. There was something dutiful in her kisses, rather than loving, and she never went out of her way to make opportunities of talking to him—except about the winding-engine. He smiled as he thought of her engrossed face, as she mastered with such determination all the intricacies of the machine. It was, of course, because she wanted to be interested in the things which *he* was interested in, and he loved her for it. He had himself been at fault, he thought, in not making more time to spend with Alice, and in not insisting on Miss Coutts effacing herself a little more, and dominating the household a little less.

As he opened the front door, Mr. Sandman made up his mind that he would talk to Alice that very night. He would go up for his usual bedtime kiss, and sit on the edge of the bed and restore between himself and his daughter their old, loving closeness. She had not mentioned the pit ponies again, and tomorrow they would be loaded aboard the railway truck and taken away. If she mentioned them, then he would explain the necessity for this, but if she didn't— and he hoped she wouldn't—then their little tiff could be forgotten, and everything would be as it was before.

Mr. Sandman hung his hat up, and turned towards the stairs. Mrs. Sandman came out of the drawing-room.

"Hullo, dear," she said, "you're back."

"Yes," he replied.

"How did your meetings go in Sheffield?"

"Not too bad. Quite successful, really."

"Oh, good, dear. You look tired. Your dinner's all ready."

"I'll just look in on Alice first."

"Have your dinner first, dear," said Mrs. Sandman. "She's sound asleep."

"Oh, is she?" said Mr. Sandman, disappointed. He still hesitated on the bottom stair.

"Besides, Mrs. Green has kept your dinner hot all this time. If it has to wait any longer, it'll be ruined."

"All right," said Mr. Sandman, and went towards the dining-room.

At the old pit-head, Dave was struggling round to the engine-house with the heavy iron wheelbarrow full of coal. He was in time to see Tommy lift the big shovel and tip one lump into the furnace and drop four outside.

"Oh, Tom!" he said. "We'll never get the pressure up at this rate."

He saw Tommy droop, and his heart misgave him.

"It's all right," he said. "I know you're doing your best.

Here, give me the shovel. You throw the lumps in by hand."

He heard a rustle and scramble behind him, and turned, and saw in the dim light Alice racing down the hollow. Dave was too much relieved to speak. He could only smile at her broadly, and Alice gave a quick smile back, and then seized a shovel and set to work.

"Now," thought Dave, heaving the wheelbarrow over to tip out the coal, "now we might just manage it."

CHAPTER FOURTEEN

As soon as they had got pressure up in the engine, Dave held a council of war squatting down by the light of the old storm-lantern which he had found in the outhouse, and filled with his mother's paraffin.

"You're sure you can manage to work the engine?" he asked Alice.

" 'Course I can! I did it when you went down before."

Dave looked only half-convinced.

"I'd leave Tommy to help you," he said, "but I'll need him down below. It'll take two of us to bring the ponies out."

"Will they be in the stables?"

"Aye, they'll've gone there when their shift is over, and Bert will have fed and groomed them. They won't have harness on, but they'll have halters, so we can just lead Flash out, and the rest'll follow, especially if Tommy comes along behind with Lion. He's a good, steady 'un."

"Won't there be people about?" asked Alice, worried. "How about the engineers?"

"They'll've gone home. And there's been no coal-getting

today, and anyway, there's no night shift. I don't think there'll be anyone down below at all."

"Will it be all dark?" said Tommy in a small voice.

And Alice quickly looked from him to Dave and said, "How will you find your way?"

"The way in from the old workings is quite close to the main roadway," replied Dave stoutly, "and there'll be lanterns that we can light along the way. Anyroad, we can follow the new machinery to the pit-bottom, and back again. No, I'm not worried about the present workings."

"How about the old workings?" asked Alice, eyeing him closely. "Dave, did you get lost last time?"

"Well—a bit—but it was all right." He stood up. "Anyway, we can follow the thread. The only thing is—"

"What?"

Dave shrugged uneasily.

"I forgot to tie it at the other end. But that won't matter, if I don't tug on it, but just follow it along."

Alice nodded. She stood up, too.

"The hard work will be the winding up at the end," said Dave. "We can only bring the ponies up one at a time. Wouldn't be safe to have more than one in the cage, in case they kick out. So be sure to keep the pressure up."

Alice nodded. Suddenly they were both nearly overcome by the responsibility of what they were trying to do, and the sheer, overpowering physical hard work. Dave glanced down and saw Tommy's face puckered with fear. He took a deep breath, and forced himself to smile, and to speak with a note of excitement instead of apprehension.

"Come on, then," he said, "the sooner we get started, the sooner they'll be out!"

Alice followed his lead and laughed and smiled.

"Yes!" she cried. "Come on!"

And Tommy suddenly looked quite happy again and jumped up and pattered off towards the shaft. Dave exchanged a sober look with Alice before following.

"I'll shout when we're ready," he said, and Alice nodded, and turned away to climb on the control platform of the winding engine.

It wasn't quite as easy to work the engine as Alice had remembered. She had to struggle very hard to force the lever into place, and for an awful moment thought she wasn't going to be able to do it, but she slammed it home at last, dropped the bolt into position and began to turn the valve. As she watched the small piece of wood dropping down to the white mark, she imagined Dave and Tommy dropping down into the darkness. She brought the cage to rest and thought of them setting out into the maze of passages. Supposing they got lost or injured? Supposing they didn't come back and she was left alone up there, not knowing what to do? She was beginning to panic, and then she remembered what Dave had said about keeping the pressure up. She hurried outside, seized the shovel, opened the furnace door and began to stoke the fire.

"Light your candle, Tom," said Dave. "Here, I'll do it for you. Now, put the matches back into your pocket. And don't take them out and drop them about all over the place. Just leave them there. You may need them."

"Yes, Dave."

As they set out, the passage seemed much blacker than before. There is no day or night below the earth, and yet the knowledge that it is dark up above as well, seems to make the darkness of the pit more extreme.

"You'd best take hold of my coat," said Dave. "And don't let go of it and start wandering about. If you lose it, just stand still and yell."

"Yes, Dave," said Tommy.

"And don't burn me backside with your candle!" said Dave.

He waited until he felt the small fingers take hold of his coat-tail, and then, holding his own candle up, he took hold of the thread and set out.

The journey was incredibly easy. Dave kept hold of the thread, being careful not to pull it, and it led them up and down, round corners and across roadways, and, long before Dave expected it, right up to the wooden barrier. The timbers were only lightly nailed together and half of them were rotten. It wasn't much trouble to pull them free and make room to climb over into the present workings.

The pit was deserted. It was strange for Dave to hold his candle up to see the coal-face, and the rails and sleepers and all of it silent and empty. He remembered his mother's words—"They'd not close the pit, would they?"—and it occurred to him that this was how it would be if Emsdale Colliery should ever be shut down. The thought gave him an old sort of shiver, like knowing what it was to be dead. He pushed it aside.

"Come on, Tom," he said. "Get on the track, and follow

the sleepers. Keep right behind me, and be ready to blow
your candle out if anyone comes."

But there was not a sign of life until they drew near to
the landing. Then there was a strange murmur and rustle
and Tommy clutched Dave and dropped his candle, which
promptly went out.

"What's that?" he said.

"Yer daft 'ap'orth!" said Dave. "It's the ponies!"

Dave banged on the nearest stall to frighten away the
mice which always scampered about after the grain.

"Come on, Flash," he said. "You're coming up above
ground. Just think of that!"

It wasn't quite as easy to get the ponies out of their
stalls as Dave had expected. People who didn't know much
about it might think it very cruel to keep the pit ponies in
underground stables, but in fact Flash and his companions
looked upon the stables as a place where they were well-
fed and comfortable after all the hard work, and they left
it with considerable reluctance, especially since their shift
had not long ended.

"Come on, Flash," said Dave. "Give a lead. Good lad."

Flash reluctantly backed out of his stall. He had often
worked a night shift, but he was well aware that on this
occasion he had not had anything like the customary rest-
time between shifts. Dave tied the halter to the ring just
outside the stables while he and Tommy fetched the other
ponies out of their stalls and assembled them in a restless
bunch.

"You stay behind with Lion," Dave commanded, and
Tommy obeyed, while Dave went to Flash and untied his
halter.

"Come on, Flash!" he said.

What Dave had forgotten, or never knew, was that Flash
as a working pit pony was very different from Flash, his
pet in the stables. Not all the miners loved the ponies as
Luke did. When Luke said "Geroff!" in that rough voice,
it was a sort of joke, and Flash knew it. But there were
other face-workers who thought of the ponies as machines
whose efficiency or inefficiency in hauling coal and returning the empty tubs affected their pay at the end of the
week. To them, a slow pony meant a hungry child, or an
ounce less of tobacco. Flash had worked for fourteen years
in the pit, and his sharp intelligence had soon taught him
that the only way to avoid a blow from a stick or the

sharp edge of a stone thrown at his rump was to use all his sturdy strength to propel himself at top speed along the roadways, his little hooves feeling the sleepers underfoot, as he instinctively bent his head to avoid sagging timbers or a low roof—instinctively, since he could see nothing in the pitch darkness of the unlighted passages.

So the moment Dave untied his halter and said, "Come on, Flash!" he was off, full speed, in the direction of the coal-face. Dave hauled on the rope in the hope of checking his speed, but in vain. Flash could pull eight hundredweight along the rails, and Dave's puny handful of pounds was no more than a thistledown to his surging energy.

"Whoa, Flash, whoa!" cried Dave, panic-stricken.

And Flash immediately stopped dead, with the other ponies jostling up behind him and Tommy squealing as he narrowly avoided Bluey's flying hooves.

"Slowly, Flash, slowly!" said Dave, hopefully, as he eased his grip of the halter.

But Flash knew only one way to travel along the roadway, and he set off again at his usual rattling pace, with Dave hanging on to the rope for dear life. The other ponies trotted briskly after, and Tommy scuttled frantically along behind, alternately clutching Lion by the halter and by the tail.

At least the main roadway was comparatively wide, and the track was in good repair. Dave nearly missed the turning to the old workings, but he just managed to check Flash in time. While the ponies milled uneasily about, Dave broke down the timbers which blocked off the narrow passage, and then carefully led Flash through the gap.

"Stand, Flash, stand!" he said, and Flash obediently did so, until his companions were assembled on the far side and Dave and Tommy had replaced the timbers as well as they could.

"There!" said Dave with satisfaction.

"They won't know how we got the ponies out, will they, Dave?" said Tommy.

"They won't," Dave replied. "No one will ever know we've been through here."

And they grinned at each other triumphantly.

"Now, Tommy," said Dave, "you be sure to keep up. I'll hold the thread, so we won't get lost."

He shone his candle around until he found the thread and took hold of it, and then he grasped Flash's halter.

"Come on, Flash," he said.

That was the last that Dave or anyone else knew of Miss Coutts' crochet thread. It was jerked out of his fingers and went down under Flash's piston-like legs, and was trampled into the wet, mucky floor by all the hooves of the following ponies. There was nothing for Dave to do but to hang on to the rope and keep going as best he could.

Fortunately, Flash did not travel as fast in the unfamiliar passages of the old workings, and it was not too difficult to keep up with him as he followed the intricate twists and turns, checked as the road divided and then shook his head and trotted briskly on.

"Does he know where he's going?" inquired Tommy, anxiously.

" 'Course he does!" said Dave. "Flash always knows where he is underground."

"He may know where he is," said Tommy, "but does he know where he's going?"

Dave didn't answer. Flash seemed very confident, but was he just taking them to some long-forgotten coal-face? Dave had expected to remember the way to the shaft, but he soon knew that he was completely lost. All he could do was to trust to Flash's instinct and hope that it was leading them to the shaft-bottom.

"It's a long way, Dave," said Tommy. "Are you sure he's right?"

"Ah, shut up, can't yer?" cried Dave, the more crossly because he was having more and more doubts himself.

Flash seemed to be pausing longer at each turning, and traveling much more slowly. Dave half expected him at any minute to come to a dead stop, confessing that he, too, had no idea where they were. Instead, as they approached a sharp turning, Flash suddenly threw his head up, and broke into a fast trot, jerking the rope out of Dave's hand.

"Whoa, Flash, whoa!" cried Dave, but he had been too much taken by surprise to speak quickly, and the other ponies, clattering after Flash, drowned his words, and knocked the candle out of his hand. In a few moments, the ponies had all vanished, and he and Tommy were alone in the darkness. He felt about for the candle, and heard Tommy stumbling towards him with a little whimper of fear.

MARKS

Mark		Example
—/	Insert em dash	Wm. Caxton ∧ /—/
—/	Insert en dash	Printing is the key∧ /–/
/;	Insert semicolon	Printing∧is the key /;
/:	Insert colon	Printing∧is the key /:
⌃⊙	Insert period	printing∧It is the ⌃⊙
!/	Insert interrogation point	Is printing the key !/
?	Query to author—in margin	Printing is the key ?
lig	Use ligature	A printing office∧ lig
sp	Spell out	Printing 1 is the∧ sp.
tr	Tr...	Prin∕∕ing is the key tr

"It's all right, Tom," said Dave, and lit a match. "Look, I'll light the candle again. We'll be all right then."

"Where are the ponies?"

"They won't've gone far."

Dave managed to light the candle, and took hold of Tommy's hand.

"Come on," he said.

They turned the corner, and Dave held up the candle. There was no sign of the ponies. Everything was dark and silent.

"We're lost, Dave, aren't we?" said Tommy, tremulously.

"No, we're not," replied Dave, stoutly.

But he thought of the maze of passages in the old workings, and his heart sank. Even if they could find their own way out, how could they ever manage to find the ponies and assemble them again? With Tommy's hand tightly clutching his, he crept along the uneven surface of the roadway. And then, halfway along the passage, he felt what Flash had felt—a breath of fresh air on his face.

"Come on!" he said, and hurried Tommy to the end of the passage and turned the corner.

There, by the shaft-bottom, stood Flash with the other ponies.

"Eh, Flash, you found it!" cried Dave, hurrying joyously towards them.

And Flash tossed his head impatiently, as though to say that he wished Dave and Tommy would get briskly about their business as he did, and not keep him waiting about.

"We're all right now," said Dave, breathless with a combination of hurrying, fear and relief. "I'll take Flash up first."

He led Flash, stumbling slightly, into the cage.

"All right, Tommy," said Dave. "Ring the bell."

Tommy reached up and pulled the handle which rang the signal bell in the engine-house. Dave, standing with Flash in the cage, waited for a few minutes, glancing upwards. Nothing happened. The cage did not move. All remained dark and silent.

"Ring it again, Tom," said Dave.

CHAPTER FIFTEEN

It had seemed a long time to Alice since the cage disappeared below the surface with the boys. She had been kept busy, of course, stoking the fire to keep the pressure up. It was very hard work on her own, and she soon became so hot that she flung off her dress and petticoat and worked on in her bodice and bloomers. But, busy as she was, she was still conscious of the time passing, and of the fact that she was all alone in the middle of the moors in the dark. As the summer night closed in about the old engine-house, she kept imagining unfriendly faces peering in at her through the black, dusty windows, and it became more and more difficult to force herself to go out and fetch more coal, with the bushes rustling so ominously about her and shadows stirring beneath the thundery sky.

"I'm not afraid, I'm not!" said Alice.

But she was. And worst of all was the thought that if the boys and the ponies were to reach the surface again, it all depended on her. Supposing the engine were to break down, or she should fail to keep the pressure up sufficiently to work the cage? Soon her hands and legs were trembling with exertion, and still she did not know whether the boys had got lost in the old workings, or been caught trying to bring the ponies out of the stables, or had got lost on the way back. She tried to think what she would do if morning came, and she still had not heard from them, and then she tried *not* to think about it, because she didn't know.

When at last the bell rang, Alice looked up at it with a

beaming smile of relief, and jumped to the controls. But either the lever had stiffened up, or else, being so tired, she no longer had the strength to slam it home. She fought and struggled with it. She turned the valve, and turned it back again, and then fought and struggled with the lever again. But, fight and struggle with it as she might, she still could not force it into place. The bell rang again, and she looked up at it despairingly.

At the foot of the shaft, Dave waited tensely in the cage, his grasp tightening on Flash's bridle.

"What's the matter with her?" he said, with a note of desperation.

"Supposing she can't work it?" said Tommy. "We'll be stuck down here, won't we? We'll be stuck down here with the ponies, until there's nothing left of us but skelingtons!"

In the old engine-house, Alice fought with the lever until the breath sobbed in her throat. She knew she couldn't move it, but she still struggled on. To have achieved so much—for Dave and Tommy to have found their way through to the stables and back again, and for the ponies to have been brought safely to the pit bottom, and now to fail because her stupid, weak, girl's hands weren't strong enough! As she wrenched and struggled with the lever, she was thinking, too, that if she couldn't work the cage, then she would have to go for help, and she could only go to her father. She couldn't leave Dave and Tommy down in the old workings, but to save them, she must betray the ponies. Once more she saw Flash and Bluey and the others driven off to be slaughtered, hustled and shouted at and bludgeoned to death, and all because of her.

Alice took a deep breath and tried to overcome her panic, and the trembling in her hands.

"I will do it, I *will!*" she said. "Oh, please, God!"

She took a fresh hold of the lever, and tried to force it home, but still it stuck on the wrong side of the ratchet. On the wall, the little piece of wood hung mockingly motionless by the lower white marking. Alice stared at it incredulously. She had failed. All that they had tried to do was destroyed. The ponies were doomed.

A voice spoke behind her.

"Want some help, then?"

Alice turned and saw Bert standing in the doorway.

"Oh, Bert!" she cried. "Oh, Bert!" and the tears ran down her cheeks.

Bert rammed the lever into place and turned the valve, and the little piece of wood rose on its string, as the cage came slowly up out of the ground. Dave, holding Flash's bridle, and watching the wet, gleaming bricks go by, could hardly believe that it was really happening, and that in a few minutes Flash would be safe. The cage came to rest, and Alice ran out to meet them.

For a moment, they could neither of them speak, and then Alice lifted the wooden bar, and Dave led Flash out of the cage.

"There!" said Alice. "There, Flash, what do you think of that?"

But Flash stumbled and almost fell.

"Hey-up, Flash!" said Dave.

He tried to lead the pony forward, but Flash floundered helplessly about.

"What's the matter with him?" said Alice, alarmed.

"I don't know," Dave replied.

It was as though Flash couldn't see where he was going. It was dark, of course, but there was light from the engine-house, and, anyway, surely ponies could see in the dark? At least as well as human beings?

"Come on, Flash," he said, and Flash stumbled again, and went down on his knees and floundered up again.

Bert had come out of the engine-house, and stood watching.

"It's all strange to him," he said. "He's not been up above ground for fourteen year."

"He'll like it when he gets used to it," said Alice.

"Yes," said Dave.

But it was not the triumphant exit which they had imagined. Flash stood and trembled, quite unlike the sturdy, self-reliant pony they were used to. Dave gave the halter rope to Alice.

"You take him," he said. "I'll go down and get another one."

He turned to go back into the cage, but paused to see Alice leading Flash down the slope which led from the pit-shaft.

"It's all right, Flash," she said, soothingly. "You're all

right. Look. Look where you're going. Oh, Flash, don't be afraid!"

But Flash lurched and stumbled helplessly down the slope, and Dave, puzzled and dismayed, stepped into the cage and lowered the wooden bar, while Bert returned to the engine-house and threw the lever.

Violet Armstrong, darning socks by the dying fire, was aware of Luke sitting motionless opposite. He was pretending to read, but the pipe he had lit half an hour before was cold in his hand, and his eyes were more often on the clock than on his paper.

"They've never been as late as this before," he said at last.

Violet didn't answer. She didn't want to show him how anxious she was herself.

"You don't think they've run away?" said Luke.

Violet stopped darning, and looked up at him.

"Now why would they do that?"

"You know why," said Luke.

They stared at each other. The old clock with the fruit painted on its face ticked away between the coronation picture of King Edward VII and Queen Alexandra and the little, faded wedding photograph of Violet and James Sadler. A last roll of thunder from the receding storm rumbled away across the moors. Luke got violently to his feet.

"I'm going to look for them!" he said. "I'll take a strap to them when I find them, frightening you like this!"

He went to the door, wrenched it open and went out. Violet sat quite still with her mending in her lap, looking at the closed door.

"Right," said Dave, as he led Lion out of the cage. "That's the last."

Alice took the halter from him and led Lion down the slope to where the other ponies were tethered to a broken-down fence, and Dave walked over to the engine-house. Bert nodded to him and closed down the engine.

"You'll have to manage now," he said. "I'm off."

"Thanks, Bert," said Dave.

Bert scowled.

"Don't tell me where you're going to put them," he

said. "I don't want to know. I haven't seen you, and if anyone asks me, I don't know where they are."

"No, Bert," said Dave.

Bert wiped his hands on a bit of rag and went outside. Dave took the lantern down and followed him. He struggled to shut the door, and Bert helped him and then they both stood for a moment looking at the dark engine-house. Except for the smoke coming from the chimney, it looked as derelict as when they had found it. Bert set off up the path, but paused, looking back.

"I'd get them away from here as soon as you can," he said. "Someone might have heard the engine."

In the drawing-room, Mr. Sandman, tired from his long day in Sheffield, was falling asleep over the evening paper, while Mrs. Sandman was diligently pulling threads in the lengths of linen which were soon to become new antimacassars. Miss Coutts had gone to bed some time before. (She was, in fact, propped up on the pillows, enjoyably plunging into the opening pages of *Rose of Castle Nair*, by A Lady.) Mr. Sandman's head jerked down, and he awoke, and grunted, and stood up.

"I think I'll go to bed," he said.

"Very well, dear," replied Mrs. Sandman. "I'll just finish pulling this thread. So tiresome. This linen is much coarser than I thought."

Mr. Sandman went out, lit the candle in the hall and took it upstairs. He was so tired that he nearly went straight into the bedroom, but he had never yet failed to say good night to Alice, or at least to smile at her while she slept, and so he opened the door of her room, lifting the latch very gently so as not to wake her. The flickering light of the candle fell on the motionless form in the bed. Mr. Sandman smiled and was about to retire. Then something odd struck him. Surely the rounded form was much too big for Alice, and—it seemed to be large all the way down, instead of curving and tapering away to legs and feet. He moved nearer and held the candle up, and then quickly pulled the sheets back, only to be confronted by the end of the bolster instead of Alice's sleeping face. He gazed at it, stunned, for a moment, and then turned and rushed out of the room, the candle flaring wildly in his hand.

"Emily!" shouted Mr. Sandman, at the top of his voice. "Emily!"

Mr. Sandman began to descend the stairs, as Mrs. Sandman came out of the drawing-room, her sewing still in her hand.

"Richard!" she said, startled. "Whatever is it? What's the matter?"

"It's Alice! She's not in her room! She's not there!"

Mrs. Sandman stared at him, confused rather than alarmed. She did not apprehend unexpected things very quickly. Another thought came to Mr. Sandman.

"Miss Coutts!" he yelled.

He started up the stairs again, quite prepared to pursue the Governess into the virgin fastnesses of her bedroom, but at that moment, just as in a Victorian melodrama, there was a heavy hammering at the front door.

Mr. Sandman ran down the stairs three at a time, and flung the door open. Sam Carter stood there, with Luke Armstrong.

"Sorry to disturb you, sir," said Sam, "but . . ."

"Have you seen my daughter?" Mr. Sandman demanded.

Sam gazed at him in astonishment.

"Your daughter? No, sir. It's the ponies. They're gone."

Mr. Sandman stared at him in silence for a moment, and then stood aside.

"You'd better come in," he said.

Sam Carter came into the hall, taking off his bowler hat, and Luke awkwardly followed him. Mrs. Sandman still stood just outside the drawing-room, quite dazed with the unexpectedness of it all.

"Well?" said Mr. Sandman, brusquely.

"This is Luke Armstrong, sir," said Sam Carter.

Mr. Sandman nodded to Luke, and then looked back at Sam. You would never have guessed it from his face, but his mind was in such a state of horror and confusion that he could hardly speak. He could see nothing but Alice's bed with the bolster in it. Where could she be? Could she possibly have run away, or had she been kidnaped? He almost turned on his heel and rushed upstairs to see if Miss Coutts was in her room, but Sam Carter was speaking again.

"Luke came to see me, to say that his two lads were

missing. And we thought they might have slipped down into the pit to say good-bye to the ponies."

Mr. Sandman stiffened. A warning bell rang in his head, but he didn't yet know what it was telling him.

"So Luke and me went down to see if we could find them. But the boys wasn't there, and neither was the ponies."

"I see," said Mr. Sandman, but he still spoke with difficulty. He was trying to listen to what Sam was saying, but so much of his mind was taken up with Alice that what remained felt very slow and stupid.

"We—er—we thought we'd get up a search-party for the boys," said Sam, "in case they've fallen down one of those old shafts up on the moors, but I thought I'd better let you know about the ponies."

"Yes," said Mr. Sandman.

Miss Coutts' voice spoke from the stairs behind him.

"I saw Alice with two boys up on the moors."

They all turned quickly, and Miss Coutts shrank back, embarrassed, aware of her blue woolen dressing-gown, and of the curler-rags in her hair.

"You saw her with two boys?" said Mr. Sandman, sharply. "Where? Where did you see them?"

"Come on, quick!" said Dave, as he struggled with Alice and Tommy to rope the ponies into three unwieldy bunches. "We must get them to the hiding-place before it gets light."

The ponies jerked and trampled about, bewildered by the strangeness of their surroundings, tossing their heads and shaking their manes in the unfamiliar fresh air.

"They'll never come with us," said Alice, worried.

"Yes, they will," Dave replied, more confidently than he felt. He took a firm grip of Flash's halter. "Come on, Flash," he said. "Give a lead."

But Flash only stumbled and floundered about, lost and uncertain, moving his head from side to side.

"What's the matter with him?" cried Dave, agonized. "Come on, Flash! Flash, what is it?"

He tried to pull him along, but Flash stumbled and nearly fell and then stood still, trembling. Dave looked at Alice in despair. She took hold of Lion's halter and led him forward.

"Come on, Lion," she said. "You lead the way."

The stout old black pony shook his head and plodded obediently forward, and the others followed.

It was a nightmare journey across the moors for Dave. Alice and Tommy called out encouragingly to the ponies as they led them along, with the occasional rumble of the retreating thunder storm rolling away behind them, but Dave walked in silence, his face set, as Flash stumbled and floundered about in the rear of the uneasy cavalcade. It was all a horrible travesty of their day-dream in which the rescued ponies danced and pranced in the sunlight, joyfully tossing their manes.

"Flash! Bluey! Sandy, True, Jester! Come, Star!"

But, instead, they slipped and stumbled in the darkness, and Flash shook his head from side to side and floundered helplessly about in the rear.

They reached the old lead mine at last, and Alice silently took hold of Flash's halter while Dave went to force the door open. The other ponies smelled the fodder and were quite ready to go inside, but even there Flash stumbled vaguely about, and Dave had to hold his halter on both sides of his head and guide him inside.

"There, Flash!" he said. "Eat some of that, and then you'll feel better."

But Flash only jerked his head back and seemed to peer from side to side.

"What do you think's the matter with him?" asked Alice.

"I don't know," said Dave. He put his arms round Flash's neck, trying to restore his confidence by the familiar touch. "It must be—after being down below all those years, everything's strange to him. He can't get used to it."

"He will soon," said Alice, "and then he'll like it. You will, Flash, won't you?"

" 'Course he will!" said Dave, and put his head down on the thick, coarse mane.

Tommy approached from the other end of the building, with a wide smile on his face. He had been too much engaged in getting Bluey and his companions safely across the moors and into the lead mine to have had much time to notice Flash's strange behavior.

"We did it, Dave, didn't we?" he said. "We saved the ponies, didn't we?"

Dave raised his head from Flash's mane, and looked at Alice, and they both laughed.

"I reckon we did!" he said.

They stood there in the great empty building, listening to the rasp and rustle of ponies pulling at fodder.

"We really did it, Dave," said Alice. "They're safe!"

The door was violently banged open. Dave, Alice and Tommy turned, alarmed. They saw in the doorway Mr. Sandman and Sam Carter, who shone a lantern in their faces.

"Alice!" exclaimed Mr. Sandman.

He took a step forward. Behind him was Luke, with Miss Coutts peering on the other side, hastily dressed, with a shawl over an untidy bundle of hair.

"Father!" cried Alice. And then, the first thought in her mind, "You won't take the ponies away, will you?"

Mr. Sandman stood motionless. He saw Alice, black-faced and tousle-haired, dressed in bodice and knickers, in company with two rough-looking and filthy pit-boys. His face hardened into deeply outraged and implacable anger.

CHAPTER SIXTEEN

EXCEPT for one light in the Armstrong house, it was quite dark in the village as Luke walked along the moorland path, with Dave on one side of him and Tommy on the other. They walked in silence, until Luke heard a little moan from Tommy. He stopped.

"What's the matter?" he asked.

Tommy gave a sniff. Luke stooped down, and saw, in the dim light of the stars, that tears were running down Tommy's cheeks.

"Eh, my little lad!" he said, and picked Tommy up and walked on.

Tommy was asleep with his head on Luke's shoulder by the time they went into the house, and Violet turned quickly towards them. She looked alarmed when she saw Luke carrying Tommy.

"Is he—?"

"Nay, he's not hurt. He's just wore out."

"Give him to me," said Violet, and took Tommy from Luke's arms and carried him upstairs. He woke up and put his arms round her neck and sobbed. "There," she said. "Come on, my bairn. You're all right now. Mother's here."

She continued up the stairs, still murmuring endearments, and Dave and Luke stood and looked at each other.

"You'd best wash your face and hands," said Luke. "Here, there's some hot water in the kettle."

He went and fetched it, and poured it into the tin bowl in the wash-house. It gave Dave an odd feeling to have Luke doing something like that. It was as though Luke knew he was too big to be carried upstairs, and so he did this for him instead.

When Dave went back into the kitchen, Luke was poking the fire into life.

"Do you want something to eat?" he asked.

Dave shook his head.

"You'd best get to bed, then."

Dave went towards the stairs, and began to climb very slowly, hardly able to move for the weight of tiredness and misery.

"Dave!" said Luke.

Dave paused, and turned to look at him. Luke didn't speak. Dave remembered when he was a little boy being frightened by a youth at the Miners' Picnic who sat and stared at him without saying anything, and how his father had told him that the boy was dumb, and that he stared because he was trying to say something, but hadn't any words. He thought that Luke looked at him in that way now.

"Go on," said Luke at last. "Get up to bed."

It was a silent breakfast in the Armstrong house next morning. Dave was feeling hungry, having missed his tea the day before, so he ate his way through the meal in a grim and dogged way. He did not want to talk about what had happened. He had even refused to speak to Tommy while they were getting dressed. It was as though he was sore all over, and if anyone touched him anywhere he would snarl like a dog.

It was not until she was passing Luke his second cup of tea that Violet said, "You'd best keep away from the pit today, Dave."

Dave looked up at her and frowned, and his mother's voice sharpened.

"The Manager could have called the police, you know, and given you in charge for stealing them ponies."

"Aye, but he didn't," said Luke unexpectedly. "He knew he'd better not!"

Dave remembered how, at the lead mine, Mr. Sandman had demanded angrily, "Are these your boys, Armstrong?" and how Luke had strode forward to stand between Dave and Tommy and turned to confront the Manager, saying, "Aye, these are my two lads," in a tone which said, "And don't you touch them, neither!"

Tommy, noisily drinking milk, put his mug down and said, "What will they do with the ponies?"

Violet looked across at Luke, and Dave and Tommy followed her gaze.

"Don't look at me!" said Luke. "The bosses never tell *us* what they're doing! I suppose the Manager'll have them fetched back and shipped off to Barnsley, same as he planned."

A deeper misery settled on Dave. So all that they had done, he and Alice and Tommy, had made no difference at all. The ponies would be killed, and it would all have been for nothing.

He managed to say, "Where will they go from?"

"The railway siding in the yard, I suppose," said Luke.

"And you stay away from there!" said Violet, sharply. "You mind what I say. I'm not having you get Luke into trouble with the Manager."

Luke pushed his chair back and stood up.

"Where's me bait-box?" he said.

Violet looked at him quickly. He often used that angry tone, but this time it sounded as though he meant it. She pressed her lips together, and got up and went in silence to fetch his tin and drinking-bottle and safety-lamp, and brought them to him. Luke took them and nodded, and she opened the door for him, and he went out. Violet stood in the doorway watching him as he walked slowly down the street, but he didn't look back. As Violet turned inside again, she became conscious of Dave's eyes on her face.

"Oh, for goodness' sake, finish your breakfast," she said, "and let me get on with my work!"

Mr. Sandman went early to the colliery that morning. He did not admit to himself that it was chiefly in order to postpone the moment when he must speak to Alice. He did not even admit that he had come to make sure that the ponies were loaded on to the truck and shipped off to Barnsley. He had given the order, and of course it would be carried out. But some terrible obstinacy made him determined to be there when it happened, and to take responsibility for it, even if he pretended all the time that he was obliged to be early at his desk, working on the figures relating to his business in Sheffield.

Steam blew violently up from the engine in the yard, alarming the ponies as Bert and some of the drivers tried to assemble them by the horse-truck. They reared back and jumped about like stiff-legged rocking-horses. Luke and the other miners, going on shift, paused to watch. Bert and the drivers tried to urge the ponies towards the ramp, but they resisted, puzzled and agitated, their small hooves clattering about. Sam Carter, deep in conversation with the Chief Engineer, glanced with a touch of anxiety from the ponies to the group of miners standing watching. He nodded to the Chief Engineer, and walked towards the miners.

"All right, lads," he said, with a slightly forced cheerfulness, "you can get below now. The machinery may take a bit of getting used to, but you can work a full shift and we'll see how we get on."

The miners made a move, but Luke stayed where he was, watching the distressed ponies. His mates, Big Alf and Amos, glanced at each other and stayed as well, and the other miners, after a few moments, stopped their drift towards the pit-head and returned to join them.

"Come on, Bert!" called Sam Carter. "Get them ponies loaded up, can't you? Take old Flash up, and then the others'll follow."

Bert tried to lead Flash up the ramp, but the pony stumbled and nearly fell. Luke suddenly stepped forward.

"Leave that pony where he is!" he said.

Bert looked at him, startled, and paused, automatically soothing the frightened pony.

"Luke, what the hell do you think you're doing?" exclaimed Sam Carter. "Get about your business, all of you! Bert, get them ponies loaded."

"No!" said Luke. "Leave them be." He looked towards the other miners. "Those ponies have served us well—helped us to win coal and gain our living. Do you think we'll let them be taken off to be slaughtered as if they were so much raw meat?"

The miners looked towards the ponies, and Bert put his hand on Flash's rough, tangled mane. Then, almost as if by accident, the men moved, slowly but purposefully, like one man, between the ponies and the horse-truck.

"Nay, Luke," said Sam, with a sudden change of tone, "think what you're doing. It's only ponies, after all."

"Is it?" said Luke. He jumped up on to the ramp, towering above the other miners. "Is it just the ponies? They're to go off to the slaughter-house because there's no use for them any more. Well. What about *us?* No one asked *us* if we wanted machinery to be put into the pit. No one told *us* how many of us would be put out of work —turned away, like Bert, because there's no use for us any more." He turned to look at Sam. "We'll not see them ponies shifted."

"I'll have to fetch the Manager to you," said Sam, threateningly.

"Fetch him, and be damned!" said Luke.

Mr. Sandman turned away from the window as Sam Carter came into his office.

"What's going on?" he demanded. "Why aren't they loading those ponies?"

"I think you'd better come, Mr. Sandman," said Sam.

Dave and Tommy had obeyed their mother so far as to stay out of the colliery yard, but if Dave had known he would be hanged for it, he could not have stayed away completely. With Tommy, he had watched, agonized, from their secret hiding-place as the ponies stumbled about the yard, and had seen Flash led towards the ramp. They were aware of Luke's intervention, though they could not hear what he said, but the movement of the miners to place themselves between the ponies and the horse-truck was unmistakable. When he saw Sam Carter setting off for the Manager's office, Dave clutched Tommy by the arm.

"Come on!" he said.

A hundred promises to his mother could not have kept him out of the colliery yard now. He and Tommy slithered down the hillside, climbed through the fence and crept round the shed in the railway siding, where Mr. Sandman, with Sam Carter beside him, was confronting Luke and the other miners. Bert stood with his hand on Flash's bridle, looking quietly pleased.

"What's going on here?" said Mr. Sandman. "When I give an order, I expect it to be obeyed. Cawsden, get those ponies loaded into the truck."

"Those ponies belong in the pit," said Luke, "same as we do."

Mr. Sandman was about to speak angrily, but he visibly controlled himself. The tone he used instead was suitable to backward children.

"The ponies," he said, very slowly and distinctly, "have been replaced by machinery, which will enable you to earn more money."

"We didn't earn more money last week," said Luke, "when we were laid off!"

The other miners murmured agreement.

"There is bound to be some dislocation," said Mr. Sandman, with immense patience, "when we are changing over from—"

"From men to machines!" Amos broke in.

"No!" said Mr. Sandman, irritated. "Not—"

"That's the 'dislocation' and we all know it!" Amos repeated. "Changing over from men to machines!"

"So it is!" roared Big Alf. "So it is, and we'll not have it!"

The other miners shouted their assent.

"We never asked for the machines!"

"We don't want 'em!"

"We'll work with the ponies, like we always have!"

Suddenly they were all shouting excitedly, the weeks of anxiety and uncertainty breaking out into anger. Sam Carter hastily stepped forward.

"Now, lads," he said, "now, lads, hear what the Manager's got to say. He's only thinking of your good—"

"Let him think of his own!" Amos interrupted. "Or he'll have no mine to manage!"

Mr. Sandman frowned. He disliked Sam's intervention, which seemed to indicate that Sam thought that he was incapable of handling the situation himself, and he resented the threat in little Amos's words. The note of conciliation, forced though it might have been, vanished from his manner, and his accent became more "London" than ever, as though he deliberately divided himself from the Yorkshiremen he was addressing.

"Now, see here, you men," he said, "the machinery is in the pit, and it is your job to work with it. I am warning you that if you don't—"

"Aye," said Luke, "and we're warning you. Get that machinery out of the pit, and get the ponies back where they belong!"

It had been a bad day for Mr. Sandman. He had gone to bed exhausted and upset, had slept restlessly, got up unrested and unhappy, and had come to work with the same black, unforgiving weight in his heart, all the worse because it was directed against Alice, and because, by some mysterious alchemy, the very love he felt for her turned his anger into a harder, blacker stone inside him. Just as a man in constant pain will sometimes be irritable, so now Mr. Sandman's temper was in a precarious state, and at Luke's words, it snapped.

"But for that machinery," he said, "the pit would probably be closed, and you out on the streets and penniless! That machinery is here to protect your livelihood, and if you weren't such damned fools, you'd realize it!"

Sam Carter's face showed his dismay. Amos looked at Luke, and at the other miners, and he threw down the pick-handle which he had collected to take on shift. He spoke quite quietly, but in the sudden silence, his words could be heard to the back of the group.

"Nay," he said, "we'll not be miscalled by the bosses."

He looked at Mr. Sandman, who glared back at him. He regretted having spoken as he had, but it would never do to show it.

"You can work your own pit, maister," said Amos, "with your own machinery, if you think it's so fine."

He turned away towards the gate, and the other men turned to follow him, throwing down pick-handles as they went. Sam Carter hurried after them.

"Now, Amos, where are you going, lad? Do you want to lose a day's pay? It's time and more you were on shift.

Go down below, lads. Come on. Let's have no more of this."

Luke, who had been moving with the others, turned to face him.

"We're on strike, Sam," he said. His eyes went past Sam Carter to Mr. Sandman, standing motionless. "And if you put those ponies into that truck," he said, "we'll never come back!"

He turned away, rejoining the other miners as they moved silently towards the pit gates. Although they had never planned it, and it appeared to have happened by accident, yet now it seemed to have an inevitability about it, and, once more, they moved as one man across the yard, away from the pit-head and out through the big iron gates.

Dave clutched Tommy as they lurked behind the corner of the shed, excited and gleeful, but awed. The whole pit idle! He felt as though he had moved a pebble and started an avalanche.

Mr. Sandman turned on his heel and walked away towards his office. Sam Carter looked after him, and then his eye met Bert's and he jerked his head.

"Best put ponies in the big shed," he said, and then paused, and finished, "for the moment."

CHAPTER SEVENTEEN

THROUGH the schoolroom window, Alice could see the big black wheels motionless against the evening sky. She, too, had had a miserable day. She spent the morning in bed. She had woken much later than usual, and heard Clara asking her mother whether she should bring Alice her breakfast in bed, but when her mother came and leaned over her, Alice pretended to be still asleep. She did not want to see anyone. She just wanted to curl up under the bedclothes with her own failure and her father's betrayal. But at lunchtime, Miss Coutts came in and poked her with a long finger.

"Come along, Alice," she said, in a much sharper tone than she had ever used before. "Get dressed and come down to luncheon."

Alice scowled up at her through tousled hair. She knew very well whose fault it was that the ponies' hiding-place had been discovered, and it had been horrible to see Miss Coutts up at the lead mine, conspiring with her father. Alice thought of defying her, but the Governess went to the door and paused.

"I shall wait here until you get up," she said.

"I'm getting up," said Alice miserably. Anything to escape Miss Coutts's company.

Alice came slowly downstairs, without any of her usual cheerful thumping from stair to stair, but Clara heard her.

"Miss Alice!" she called, in a conspiratorial voice.

She drew Alice into the passage outside the kitchen.

"Have you heard the news?"

"What news?"

"There's a strike, up at t'pit."

"A strike!"

"Over the ponies," said Clara, full of suppressed excitement. "Luke Armstrong said they'd not go down the pit unless the ponies went down, too, and the others backed him up, and so there's a strike. Ee, I'll wager the master is fair moithered with it all!"

"Yes," said Alice.

Clara looked rather disappointed.

"Well, I'll serve dinner, then, Miss Alice, now you're down."

"Lunch," said Alice. "We call it lunch."

Mr. Sandman did not come home at mid-day. He was busy with Sam Carter and the Deputies and the Engineers, arranging for the maintenance of the pit and the machinery during the strike, and sent a message for a slice of pie and a pint of ale to be sent over to his office. So Alice's lunch was nearly as silent as Dave's breakfast, with Miss Coutts in a chilly triumph of disapproval, and Mrs. Sandman quite cowed by it. Alice's feelings were divided between thankfulness for the ponies' reprieve and anxiety for her father. She knew how much it meant to him that he should make a success of his new post, and she hated to think that she had made difficulties for him. She longed to tell him how sorry she was, and all through the long afternoon of lessons, she planned what she would say to him. Miss Coutts went out of the room after tea, leaving Alice struggling with her writing exercise. "Punctuality is the politeness of Kings," Alice wrote over and over again in a spidery hand interspersed with very unregal blots. As soon as her father came in, she would run downstairs and put her arms round his neck and say, "I'm sorry, I'm sorry!" And then he would tell her all about the strike, and she would be able to ask him about the ponies, and perhaps they would find a way to save them and the miners would go back to work, and everything would be all right. "Punctuality is the politeness of Kings," wrote Alice, for the fiftieth time, and put her pen down and leaned forward to look at the winding wheels, motionless against the evening sky.

Miss Coutts opened the door.

"Alice," she said, "your father wishes to see you in the drawing-room."

"Oh, is he home?" cried Alice, starting up, delightedly. "I didn't hear him!"

She set off for the door.

"Alice," said Miss Coutts. "Put your pen away, and close the ink-stand. Your fingers are covered with ink. Go and wash your hands and comb your hair. You are certainly not going to see your father in that condition."

By the time Alice went downstairs, with Miss Coutts leading the way, she felt like a criminal in the custody of a warder, and she felt it even more when she went into the drawing-room and saw her father sitting facing her in an upright chair, like a judge. Mrs. Sandman sat in her chair by the fireplace, and seemed to be trying to look as though she were not there at all.

"Come in, Alice," said Mr. Sandman.

There was no question of flinging her arms round his neck. Alice could only stand in front of him as if she was in the dock, while Miss Coutts stood guard in the doorway.

"Well, Alice," said Mr. Sandman, after an impressive

pause, "I hope you've had time to think over your behavior, and are thoroughly ashamed of yourself."

Now, it is one thing to volunteer an apology, and quite another thing to have someone endeavor to extract it. Alice accordingly said nothing, but looked down at the carpet and frowned slightly. Mr. Sandman's voice hardened.

"Thanks to you," he said, "I have a strike on my hands —you and those colliery brats who ought to be in a reform school!"

Alice looked up at him quickly and then down again. That he could speak of Dave and Tommy in that way opened such a chasm between them that she felt that they could never really meet and talk to each other again.

"I hold myself partly to blame," Mr. Sandman continued, "for having encouraged you to take an interest in things which were quite unsuitable for a little girl of your age. I have talked it over with Miss Coutts, and I agree with her that what you need is a firm hand and much more supervision. From now on, you will spend your time with your Governess, learning the things which a young lady ought to know, and which will improve your character and give you a little self-discipline."

Alice could feel Miss Coutts' smug expression right through the back of her head.

"I'm not going to punish you," said Mr. Sandman. "I hope it will be enough punishment for you to know that I am very angry and disappointed in you. And I hope that your future behavior will show that you understand what you have done, and are very sorry for it."

Mr. Sandman paused, expectantly. Alice looked at the pattern on the carpet.

"Well?" said Mr. Sandman. "What have you to say?"

Alice looked up at him.

"What will happen to the ponies?" she asked.

She heard her mother catch her breath, but she kept her eyes on her father's face. He looked steadily back at her, and when he spoke, his voice was very calm and controlled.

"You had better go to bed now," he said.

Alice prepared to go.

"You may kiss your mother good night."

Alice thought that her mother would have liked to say something as she kissed her, but she glanced at Mr. Sandman, and just gave a little nervous smile. As Alice passed her father on her way to the door, he held up his cheek for a penitent kiss. Alice paused, looked at him without speaking, and then walked straight out of the room.

Mr. Sandman sat in silence for quite a long time, while Mrs. Sandman took up her drawn thread work. He fidgeted slightly, and then stood up.

"I think I'll get a breath of fresh air," he said.

"All right, dear. Don't be too long. It's almost dinnertime."

Mr. Sandman went out of the front door, and sighed. He looked towards the winding wheels still faintly etched against the darkening sky. He was right, absolutely right. He had almost worked himself to death to save the colliery, and now the men, for whose sake he had done it, had repaid him with insult and ingratitude. And Alice, towards whom he had always been the kindest and most considerate of fathers, had publicly disgraced him, and had then refused to apologize, and had openly defied him. He had spoken to her reasonably—yes! reasonably and—and with the utmost toleration!—and yet she had not responded in any way. He stood there in the garden, listening to the quiet rustle of the shrubbery and to the occasional twitter of nesting birds. For a man who was so entirely in the right, it was strange that he felt so utterly miserable.

"Will the Union give you their backing?" Violet asked Luke next morning.

"They might," he answered.

"And then again they might not. And if they don't, we don't get any strike pay. What are we going to live on?"

Luke, sitting by the fire in his shirtsleeves, glanced up at her, but said nothing. Violet put the teapot on the table with a heavy thump as Dave came clattering cheerfully down the stairs.

"I don't know what you've got to look so cheerful about," said Violet. "You won't be grinning when there's nothing to put on the table for your dinner!"

Dave looked surprised.

"Aren't you glad they're not going to kill the ponies?"

"Ponies, ponies!" cried Violet. "I'm sick and tired of the ponies! That's all you think about! Ponies won't put food in your belly or clothes on your back! Come on.

You'd best have your breakfast while there's still something to eat in the house."

Dave, puzzled by his mother's inexplicable bad temper, sat down, and Violet returned to the stove to take the eggs and bacon out of the pan.

"Luke," she said, "you can have your breakfast, and then get out of my way. I'm not having you under my feet all day. If you're 'on strike,' you can go and be on strike somewhere else!"

To Dave's astonishment, Luke got meekly up and came to sit in his place at table. As he did so, he caught Dave's eye. And, although neither of them spoke, they did, in fact, communicate directly for the first time since Luke had married Dave's mother. And what they said was, "Women! You never know what they'll be up to next!" Dave hastily looked down at the table, but not before he hàd seen a tiny, hastily suppressed grin on Luke's face, and had answered it with a tiny, hastily suppressed grin of his own.

Violet banged their plates down in front of them and went to the foot of the stairs.

"Tommy!" she called. "I'm not going to tell you again!"

As she turned away, there was a knock at the street door. Luke half rose, but Violet was already there. She opened the door to Amos, and stood eyeing him severely.

" 'Morning, Amos," she said, with a grim note in her voice.

Dave thought that Amos, too, caught the warning signal. He nodded ingratiatingly.

"Good morning, Violet. Er—is Luke there?"

Violet stood aside in silence, and Amos came inside. He looked towards Luke, who had gone on eating his breakfast as though he wasn't particularly concerned. But now he turned round in his chair.

"Well?" he said.

Amos still paused for a moment before answering.

"The Union won't back us," he said at last.

Luke's face showed that this was a blow. He put his knife and fork down. Violet seemed to be waiting for him to speak, but when he didn't, she did.

"Then we don't get any strike pay," she said.

In the silence which followed, Tommy came clattering merrily downstairs.

"Me bootlace broke," he said, "and I couldn't get it tied up."

.He reached the bottom of the staircase with a bright smile on his face, but as he became aware of Luke, Amos and Violet looking at each other without speaking, and of Dave sitting very still, his look of cheerfulness slowly faded.

"Sit down and have your breakfast," said Violet, but she didn't sound angry any more. Rather it was as though she saw a long and weary road ahead of them.

CHAPTER EIGHTEEN

THE ponies were in the big shed beside the railway siding, not far from the pit-head. It wasn't as convenient as their own stables in the pit, but Bert and the boys had done their best to make it comfortable, with fodder and hay and buckets of water. When the boys arrived on the first day of the strike, Bert was examining Flash's eyes, holding the noseband on each side, and peering at him closely.

"What is it, Bert?" asked Dave, anxiously. "What's wrong with him?"

"Nay," said Bert, releasing Flash and shaking his head, "to think I never realized it before. He's got anthracitis. He can't see, no more than a mole."

Dave gazed back at him, stricken.

"You mean, he's blind?"

"I reckon so. When he was down in the pit, he knew his way about, so nobody noticed."

Bert turned away.

"Come on, Tommy. Are you going to help me get some more hay, then?"

Tommy scampered readily off, but Dave put his arms round Flash's neck. He had loved Flash dearly when he was active and self-reliant and aggressive. Now that he was blind and helpless, Dave loved him still more.

Up on the iron balcony outside the Manager's office, Mr. Sandman stood with Sam Carter and one of the Deputies. His eyes were on the small group of men who stood outside the gates. They were the pickets—miners who took it in turns to stand guard and make sure that no one came to work without realizing that there was a strike. In so small a colliery, and with its workers almost entirely housed in Emsdale village, this was hardly likely, but still the Miners' Union conducted its business according to a ritual as rigid as the service of the Church of England or the doctrine of the Baptists' Chapel, and even an unofficial strike had to obey the rules.

"When does the owner get back, sir?" inquired Sam Carter.

"I'm not sure," Mr. Sandman replied, his eyes still on the desultory gathering outside the colliery gates. "His Lordship has gone abroad, but the Agent thought that he would be returning in a couple of weeks or so."

There was another silence.

"He's not going to be pleased," remarked Sam, "not with his having spent all that money on machinery, and now the pit idle."

Mr. Sandman had noticed before Sam Carter's exasperating habit of putting into words thoughts which you would much rather he had left unsaid.

"I daresay," he replied, brusquely.

Sam cleared his throat, and Mr. Sandman realized that there was something else he wished to say, and that he was advancing towards it. Sam sometimes reminded Mr. Sandman of an old sheepdog who took a few steps forward, lay down, took a few more, slithering along on the grass, glanced around, took a few paces more, until at last he arrived at the heels of the sheep he wanted to harry.

"Er—have you any ideas, sir, about—er—how to end the strike?"

Mr. Sandman turned to look him in the eye.

"Certainly," he said. "The strike will be ended when the men are prepared to go back to work again—and they had better not leave it too long."

He turned on his heel and went into his office and closed the door.

Mr. Sandman stayed in his office all day, except for a grimly formal lunch, with Alice silent, and Mrs. Sandman twittering nervously, and Miss Coutts making "polite conversation" which froze all natural communication like icicles on an outdoor pump. One by one, the sharp splinters of information or platitude were proffered, broken off and laid aside, and Mr. Sandman, who seemed to have become a sort of unwilling accomplice in some mysterious plot, found himself answering, smiling at and agreeing with Miss Coutts as though they were alone in the room.

"Well, my dear," he forced himself to say at last, with a desperate smile towards his wife at the other end of the table, "you're very quiet. What have you been doing?"

"Oh," said Mrs. Sandman, starting nervously, as though she were being accused of some crime, "nothing."

"Well, Alice and I have managed to keep ourselves busy, haven't we?" said Miss Coutts, brightly.

Alice kept her eyes on her plate. Mrs. Green, as though to add to the funereal atmosphere, had graced the table with tough cold mutton, followed by a slightly undercooked plum duff—a pudding which at the best of times has a tendency to look like a small corpse, and at the worst of times can taste like it, too.

"Alice!" said Mr. Sandman, sharply, "answer your Governess when she speaks to you."

Alice looked up at him. As Mr. Sandman met the gaze of those great brown eyes with their look of hurt incredulity, he felt a sharp pain himself, but, perversely, it only confirmed him in his unyielding determination. He might have considered giving way to *her* pain, perhaps, but not to his own. But before Alice could speak, Miss Coutts interposed with fine magnanimity. It *was* magnanimous, but the trouble was, she made it so clear that she *thought* it was, and also it seemed as though she once more came between Alice and her father.

"I thought we would take a little walk this afternoon," said Miss Coutts, "and blow the cobwebs away. You'll like that, Alice, won't you?"

"Yes, Miss Coutts," said Alice, and looked down at her plate and reluctantly poked the pallid suet pudding.

"I really think," said Mrs. Sandman, "that this pudding

is not very nice. Mrs. Green seems to have let the water get into the cloth. Alice, dear, don't eat it if you don't fancy it."

"Thank you, Mother," said Alice, and tears came into her eyes at the kind tone, and even more at the thought that she felt grateful for it—she who had been used to kindness and affection from her mother and her father every day!

Mr. Sandman walked back to the colliery, passing the picket on the gates, now reduced to two men, who glanced at him with a hint of uneasiness and, after a moment's hesitation, touched their caps to him. Mr. Sandman nodded to them curtly, and walked across the deserted yard to his office. It was difficult to concentrate in the silence, without the bang and rattle of a working pit all about him—the clatter of hooves and rumble of colliery drays, the sound of shovels, the hammering of iron from the smithy, the occasional shouts and an awereness of the constant movement of the winding-wheels. But Mr. Sandman bent doggedly over his papers, trying to work out how long he could have the pit idle and still meet the commitments he had made. Fortunately, his series of skirmishes with the engineers had gained some extra time. The job had been completed sooner than he had secretly expected. And with the small stock of coal accumulated during the past weeks—Mr. Sandman found his thoughts wandering again. Supposing Alice never did apologize? Could he bring himself to say that he forgave her anyway, and would it be right to do so? He knew that when she really set her mind, she was as obstinate as—well, as anyone could be—and suddenly he found himself shying away from the horrible thought that their loving, close relationship might be gone forever, and that never again would they be able to feel for each other what they had felt before. It was a relief to straighten up, shake himself and bend once more with determination over the sheets of calculations on his desk.

While Mr. Sandman was toiling away in his office, such is the injustice of life that the men whose livelihood he was endeavoring to preserve were cheerfully disporting themselves up on the moors with whippet-racing. It seemed as though every man who lived in Emsdale was there, their indignant wives having swept and dusted them out of their houses like so many hooked rugs. They didn't often get out on the moors on a weekday, and there was a holiday atmosphere, somewhere between a fair and a picnic. Tommy and Dave had gone there, with the other boys from the village, and jumped about excitedly as final bets were made, and the dogs put into the "traps." Pearl was to take part in this race, and since she was the only bitch, and smaller than the other dogs, Luke had no trouble in finding takers for his bets.

"Nay, Luke," said Big Alf, "I know Pearl's a good bitch, but she's not as young as she was."

"Give you two to one," said Luke.

"Done!" said Big Alf.

"I've got a ha'penny on her!" said Tommy, as he helped Luke to put Pearl into the crate.

"Have you?" said Luke. "She'd better win, then," and he gave Dave a wink.

Dave nearly winked back, but didn't quite. Still, everything did seem different out there on the moors, and Luke seemed much younger, somehow, as he did in the old days when he used to lark about with their father, kicking a football down the valley at the back of the houses, or vaulting the fence into the field.

"Come on, my lads!" he cried, easing the sliding door down on its bit of string. "You've met your match now. Pearl'n me'll soon have your money off you!"

There was a derisive jeer from his mates, and Luke jeered back, laughing, and Dave and Tommy joined him, with Amos and the other miners who had put money on Pearl's winning.

Alice, plodding along a nearby moorland path in the custody of Miss Coutts, saw what was going on. Her face lit up, and she stopped to watch. There was a sudden burst of power and energy as the whippets were released from the traps. The miners roared encouragement.

"Come on, Blackie! Duke! Come on, Duke!"

"Come on, Pearl!" cried Dave and Tommy. "Come on! Pearl! Come on!"

"Sonny!" roared Big Alf. "What's the matter with yer? Come on, Sonny!"

It was over almost before they had time to yell. Pearl streaked out of the trap after the hare's skin which had set off ahead of them, wound along the ground on a taut string, and although the other whippets followed in almost simultaneous flashes of brown, gray and cream, the lead she had gained in her adroit emergence from the trap was enough to give her the victory.

"She won! She won!" cried Tommy, and did his usual tumbling handstand to celebrate.

"She won!" Alice whispered, from her vantage-point nearby. "Pearl won!"

Miss Coutts, a townee from the crown of her straw hat to the soles of her buttoned boots, had not at first realized what was going on, but even she could not mistake the cheers and groans, and the sight of money changing hands.

"Alice!" she exclaimed. "I believe it is those dreadful miners! And they are—I do believe they are *betting* on a dog race. Well! I never saw anything so shocking in my life. They are supposed to be on strike, and yet they have the impudence to be seen out here playing with their dogs!"

"They've nothing else to do," said Alice, "and besides," she added, breaking into purest Yorkshire, as she quoted Dave, "you have to keep a whippet exercised, you know."

One of the miners, glancing up, saw the two figures on the nearby path.

"Isn't that Manager's daughter?" he said.

The others turned to look, pausing in their settling of debts and collecting of dogs.

"Aye," said another, "and a game little lass she must be, too."

Miss Coutts observed with alarm that she and her charge had attracted the men's attention.

"Quick, Alice!" she said, "Come away. They might attack us!"

And seizing Alice's arm, she hurried her away along the path, giving her no time to do more than exchange a quick, despairing glance with Dave over her shoulder.

"Here you are, Luke," said Big Alf. "She only beat Sonny by a head."

"I daresay," Luke replied, cheerfully pocketing the money, "but that head's enough to cost you two bob."

"Here, Luke, here's mine," said George Arbuthnot, coming up.

But this time Luke hesitated, and then did not hold out his hand.

"Keep it for the moment, George," he said. "You can

pay me when the strike's over." And then he added, with mock fierceness as he saw his friend's grateful look, "And don't think I won't remember and have it off you!"

Luke carefully selected two pennies from his winnings and held one out to Tommy.

"Here, Tommy," he said, "that's for you."

"Thank you, Luke," said Tommy, delighted.

Luke held the other penny out to Dave. Dave shook his head.

"No."

"Come on, lad," said Luke, smiling. "You earned it fair and square."

"I don't want it," said Dave.

Dave was thinking about George Arbuthnot, and that money would be short during the strike, and shouldn't be wasted on things like licorice sticks and gob-stoppers. But he didn't say so, and Luke's smile vanished as he put the money back in his pocket and turned away.

"Oh, suit yourself!" he said, angrily.

It might seem to Miss Coutts, seeing the miners out on the moors on a windy, sunny day with their whippets, that a strike was, after all, nothing less than a stolen holiday. But in the village it assumed a very different aspect. Just as the colliery, with its empty yard and static wheel, had an unnatural air, so, too, there was something ominous and unfamiliar about Emsdale. There were more people about than usual, since the men were there as well, but there was nothing bustling or prosperous about the village street, as the men squatted on doorsteps or lounged on corners, smoking their pipes and talking in a desultory way. It was like the onset of an illness, when the patient hardly knows what is wrong, but is aware of an indefinite malaise, and knows it will get worse. Soon the pipes were kept more often in the pocket than in the mouth, and Mrs. Binks, the hard-featured woman who kept the General Goods and Grocery Store, put a large notice in the window which read NO CREDIT.

"That woman!" said Violet Armstrong, serving out an Irish stew which consisted chiefly of potatoes and carrots, with a few pieces of scrag-end of mutton. "She'd rather say 'no' than 'yes' any day. I believe if you offered her a thousand pound, she'd say 'no' first, and 'yes' afterwards."

Tommy poked about in his plate with his fork.

"I haven't got any meat," he said.

"Here," said Luke.

He took his largest and meatiest bone between his knife and fork, and conveyed it on to Tommy's plate.

"No, Luke, you need it!" cried Violet.

"I've got all I need," said Luke.

Dave looked quickly between him and Violet.

"I don't want any," he said.

"Eat what you've got, and be thankful," said Violet. "There's little enough. I've shared it out fairly."

They ate in silence for a while.

"It's the Arbuthnots I worry about," said Violet. "Seven children, and he was laid up for three months last year, after that accident. I saw Ada at the shop this morning. They haven't got a penny put by. And they're not the only ones. There are plenty more like them."

Dave looked up quickly.

"But they'd not give up the ponies, would they?" he asked.

Luke looked across at Violet, and there was defiance in his voice when he answered.

"Nay," he said. "They'd not."

For the next two weeks, life crept on in the same state of half-suspended animation. Women ransacked old teapots for the last few shillings, hoarded for the boys' new boots or to buy the dresses, caps and aprons for the girl to take with her into service. Men slipped out at night, to do some poaching, or to dig some coal from a seam which ran near the surface by Napp's Hill. Mr. Sandman went grimly each day to his office, past increasingly surly pickets. Miners and Manager were like two wrestlers, both helpless, yet each with a hold he did not mean to let go. It was as though they were all waiting for something to happen to release them, without in the least knowing what that something was.

Then Mr. Sandman received a letter from the Agent, saying that Lord Harrogate had returned from Baden-Baden, and had requested that Mr. Sandman should wait upon him at his convenience—or rather, next morning, which happened to be Lord Harrogate's convenience, but which he evidently felt was the same thing.

It was with an uneasy heart that Mr. Sandman climbed up into the trap. There may be a Manager somewhere in the world who can with equanimity confront the owner of his colliery and inform him that the pit is closed, and that the expensive machinery which he has purchased is lying idle, but Mr. Sandman was not that man. He knew that he had done only what was reasonable, and in accordance with the wishes of any reasonable colliery owner. But whether he had done it *in the best way* was the little, niggling uncertainty which made him prepare to face Lord Harrogate with far less assurance than he might otherwise have mustered. As he drove across the park, he could not help asking himself whether, if Alice had not been involved in the affair, he might have handled it a little better, and avoided the strike altogether. A drizzle of rain began to fall when he was halfway there, and handing to the butler a pair of sodden gloves and a dripping hat, he felt his self-confidence still further diminished by that great man's obvious reluctance to put these objects down on a well-polished table.

"His Lordship is in the study, sir," said the butler, and trod across the marble hall, followed by Mr. Sandman who made damp footmarks all the way.

Lord Harrogate appeared to be engrossed in some delicious occupation at his desk, but paused when he heard the butler's announcement, hesitated, and with obvious regret, abandoned it to greet his Manager.

" 'Morning, Sandman," he said. " 'Morning. Come in, come in. What did you want to see me about?"

"Er—" Mr. Sandman thought of explaining that it was not he who had sought the meeting, but decided against it. "I wished to inform you, m'Lord," he said, "about the strike at Emsdale Colliery."

"*Strike?*" Lord Harrogate exclaimed. "What the devil have they got to strike about? I'm the one who's losing money. *I'll* go on strike one of these days, and then they'll be sorry!"

Mr. Sandman smiled, happy to find His Lordship in such a jovial mood.

"Yes, my Lord," he said. "Er—"

But Lord Harrogate's attention had wandered back to the desk.

"Have you seen one of these things?" he inquired, picking up a stout black tube with silver trimmings. "It's a pen. You see, you dip it in the ink-stand, and pull this lever down, and—you won't believe this—it actually fills with ink."

"Really, my Lord?" said Mr. Sandman, politely.

Lord Harrogate withdrew the pen from the ink-stand. He found that his fingers were covered with ink, and hastily wiped them on his handkerchief, and stuffed it away again.

"Now, you see," he said, "you can use it for hours— days—and scribble away—don't have to keep dipping it in the ink. Splendid idea. Splendid!"

He drew a sheet of embossed writing paper towards him, and eagerly approached it with the fat silver nib. Before he could write anything, a huge black blot fell with a splash on to the pure white expanse.

"Damn!" said Lord Harrogate, and with the start of surprise which he gave, three more blots splattered down. "Damn!" said Lord Harrogate again.

He put the pen down, and wiped his hands again on his handkerchief. His mood was not quite as jovial as it had been.

"Well?" he said. "What is it this time? They want more money, I suppose, as usual?"

"No, my Lord," said Mr. Sandman. He hesitated. "It is more a question of the—er—machinery."

"*Machinery?*" Lord Harrogate exclaimed. "You don't mean that after I paid all that money to buy machines, the men are refusing to use them?"

"Oh no, my Lord," replied Mr. Sandman. He hesitated again, and added, "Not exactly."

"Well, what is it, then?" inquired Lord Harrogate, with a hint of impatience. "Sit down, sit down."

He went to sit behind the desk, and Mr. Sandman perched on the edge of an upright chair, and cleared his throat.

"The trouble chiefly concerns the pit ponies."

He had a feeling of incredulity as he said the words. Was he really sitting there, in the study of Harrogate House, trying to explain to his noble employer that his colliery had come to a halt because of a handful of entirely replaceable animals, many of them past their working best?

"You see, the men—"

"Just a minute," Lord Harrogate interrupted. "I thought it was agreed that we would replace the ponies with machines."

"Yes, indeed," Mr. Sandman said. "That has been done. We have installed a main-and-tail hauler, and the men will manhandle the tubs to and from the face."

"Well?" demanded Lord Harrogate again. "Doesn't it work?"

It went fleeting through Mr. Sandman's mind that Lord Harrogate had had more than one experience with machinery of one sort and another which did not work.

"Oh, it works perfectly well, my Lord," he said, hastily. "That is, it—it will. But it appears that the men are concerned in case the replacement of the pit ponies might be followed by a reduction of the number of men employed."

"Hm," said Lord Harrogate.

Mr. Sandman wasn't quite sure whether or not His Lordship was listening. He cleared his throat again.

"I think the truth is that the men would like to have an assurance that . . ."

"The men would *like?*" Lord Harrogate repeated. For the first time, he gave Mr. Sandman his undivided attention, and the effect was terrifying, as the dangerous lion's strength of power and riches showed through that deceptive amiability. "I am not interested in what the men would like. They are there to work, and you are there to see that they do it."

Mr. Sandman opened his mouth and shut it again.

"You told me, Sandman, that this machinery would make the colliery pay. Now you tell me that the men don't want to use it."

"It is not quite that, my Lord. It is more that—"

Lord Harrogate held up his hand, and Mr. Sandman fell silent.

"*You* can tell *them* that unless they go back to work, I shall close the pit, and use the land for shooting."

Mr. Sandman tried not to show the shock that he felt.

"Yes, my Lord," he said. He gathered his wits together. "I understand perfectly. But perhaps if you would authorize me to give the men an assurance . . ."

But Lord Harrogate had risen, and was coming round the desk.

"I'm sorry, Sandison," he said. "There is nothing more to say."

Mr. Sandman rose to his feet. Lord Harrogate continued on his way to the door, and opened it.

"Nothing at all," he said, and went out.

CHAPTER NINETEEN

Luke Armstrong sat on the doorstep of the house, and Amos squatted beside him. Other miners sat or squatted outside the houses, but there was an odd silence in the village. They might have been figures in a Dutch painting —out there to give some sign of life, but not really living. Life in human beings is movement and bustle and speech. They had nothing to say, and nowhere to go. That surge of activity which took place morning and evening, to the pit, and back again, was like the surge of blood through the heart, and without its beating, there was a kind of death in the village, and in the men who sat sucking empty pipes on its doorsteps.

Luke took out his tobacco pouch, and felt in it. He turned it upside down in his hand, and three flakes of tobacco fell out. Amos, having nothing else to do, was watching him, and Luke, putting the pouch away, and carefully placing the three flakes of tobacco in his pipe, became aware of it, and looked up, and gave a rueful grin. Then he saw something in the street.

"Hey-up!" he said.

Amos followed his gaze. Sam Carter was walking from the direction of the pit, a piece of paper in his hand.

"Now, what does Sam Carter want, I wonder?" said Amos.

They could hear the sound of Sam's footsteps on the cobbles in the silent street, as the miners sat and watched him. He paused outside the Drover's Arms, the public house which also did duty as the Miners' Welfare Club. Apparently unaware of the many eyes upon him, Sam pinned the piece of paper on the notice-board beside the entrance to the Public Bar. He stood back to examine it, was not quite satisfied, moved one of the drawing-pins to make it straighter, and then, after a final glance, turned and walked away again towards the colliery.

There was no rush towards the notice, standing out white and glaring against the dingy board. The miners sat on where they were, watching Sam Carter's sturdy figure walking away up the street. Amos was the first to stand up. He looked down at Luke.

"Coming?"

Luke shrugged and stood up.

"May as well."

In twos and threes the miners strolled casually up to the Drover's Arms, and lace curtains twitched as the women peered out of the windows. Amos got there first, and turned, a broad grin on his face.

"Manager's given in!"

"What? What does it say?"

They all gathered round, jostling to read the notice, and Dave, slithering down the path from the moor, ran to join the group.

"He's called a meeting at the pit!" he heard George Arbuthnot exclaim.

"Ah well," said Big Alf, "only to be expected. We knew he'd not want the pit idle for long."

"Nay, it's more than his job's worth," said one of the others.

They began to move off, smiling broadly, as Dave ducked under their elbows to read the notice. Luke stood still for a moment, and drew a deep breath of relief, and then began to walk towards the colliery.

"What does it mean?" called Tommy, hurrying up to Dave.

Dave's face was glowing with pleasure.

"It means we've won," he said. "The ponies are safe!"

Sam Carter, with one of the Deputies, stood outside the Manager's office, but the miners were all assembled before Mr. Sandman stepped outside, and came to stand facing them, his hands resting on the iron railing. Dave and Tommy, racing along the path at the back of the yard and climbing, breathless, through the fence, saw Bert standing outside the shed and crept round the corner to join him. The men's faces were cheerful, and they glanced at each other and smiled as they waited for Mr. Sandman to speak.

"All right," he said, "I shan't keep you long."

The miners glanced at each other, and Dave saw Luke frown. The tone of Mr. Sandman's voice was not the tone one would expect from a Manager who was about to propose peace terms agreeable to both parties.

"Either you go back to work tomorrow," he said, "or else the pit closes—for good."

There was a gasp, and then a few laughs. Mr. Sandman's voice cut sharply through the general murmur.

"I mean what I say."

This time the men did not glance at each other. They stopped laughing, and kept very still, their eyes on Mr. Sandman's face.

"There is only one way this colliery can be made to pay," said Mr. Sandman, "and that is by the use of machinery. If you will go back to work, and learn to use the machines to your advantage, so that you can earn more money, then I promise you that all the men who have have been made idle will get taken on again. And the night shift will be started again as soon as you have become accustomed to mechanization, and as soon as the coal is being fetched out in reasonable quantities."

He paused. The miners shuffled uneasily.

"We've heard all that before," said Luke. "It's only promises."

"Aye, so it is!"

Mr. Sandman's voice once more broke into the growing murmur of discontent.

"Very well, then, I will give you something more than promises—I will give you an assurance."

The men were silent, their eyes fixed once more on Mr. Sandman's face.

"I have obtained an offer from the owners of a steelworks to take all our coal for the whole year, on contract."

There was a brief silence.

"On contract?" said Big Alf.

"That's right."

"Then we'd be assured of work for the whole year."

"Yes," said Mr. Sandman. "But it must be cheap coal. That means hard work, and making good use of the machinery."

"It'd be worth it, though," said George Arbuthnot, "to be sure of money coming in all year round."

"How about the ponies?" called Luke.

When Mr. Sandman replied, his face and voice were quite expressionless.

"There is no place for ponies in this pit."

Dave noticed with alarm that, although the miners shifted uneasily on their feet, there was no outcry at his words—not even a murmur.

"It's a simple choice," said Mr. Sandman, after a moment. "Full employment, and, I hope, prosperity for all of you, or else closure of the pit, and ruin. I leave it to you to decide."

"There's only one way we can decide!" said Big Alf.

Mr. Sandman permitted himself a faint smile of satisfaction, and Dave, seeing it, despaired.

"Wait a minute!" Luke shouted, stopping a slight, general move, as though the meeting was over. "We're not making up our minds, just like that. We want to think it over."

Dave thought he caught a note of desperation in Luke's voice, too. It was odd to stand on the outskirts of the crowd, and to feel that he and Luke were—almost—partners, just the two of them, trying to save the ponies. Tommy, watching wide-eyed, hardly knew what was going on, and Bert, whatever he felt, had spent too long in the pit, doing what he was told. He would never disobey the masters. Only Luke was there to make this desperate last stand against the Manager, and even against his own mates.

"Nay, Luke, lad!" said Big Alf.

"We don't go back after a strike without we hold a meeting of our own," said Luke. "You know that."

The mood of the miners changed. Luke had appealed to the hard-won rights and customs of the Miners' Union, and that was something they could not ignore.

"Aye, well, that's right enough," said Big Alf, and there was a general murmur of agreement.

"We'll hold our own meeting," said Luke, "and talk it over."

Dave saw the annoyance on Mr. Sandman's face, and saw Sam Carter glance from him to Luke. He remembered what his mother had said about getting Luke into trouble with the Manager, and for the first time he felt uneasy about it. But when Mr. Sandman spoke, he addressed them all.

"Very well," he said, coldly. "But I want to know, within the hour, whether or not you are going back to work."

He turned away, and went into his office.

They held the meeting behind the shed, with the ponies shifting about in the straw, and Bert, Dave and Tommy standing listening just inside the doorway.

"We've got to go back, we know that," said George Arbuthnot.

"But not just on *his* terms!" cried Luke. He looked round the faces staring unresponsively back at him. "Ah, come on, lads! We struck for the ponies, but it wasn't just that. We struck for a bit of respect for us and our work. If they can turn ponies out without a thought or a word, they can turn men out, too. If we go back just on his say-so, without making terms . . ."

Alf cut in, harshly.

"How *can* we make terms?" he said. "It's a colliery village, and we live in colliery houses!"

"Aye," said George Arbuthnot. "If the pit closes, then we're out on the streets, every one of us, and our wives and bairns. No money, nowhere to live, no food and no work."

"And nowhere to find none, neither," said Amos. "There's not a pit in Yorkshire that hasn't got some men idle."

Luke turned to look at him. Amos looked back at him, guilty, but defiant.

"Nay, Luke, lad," he said. "If the colliery closes, we're done for. Think on."

"And how if we go back to work, and find that half of us are laid off because the machines are doing our work instead?" said Luke.

"It'd still be better than all of us out of work, and our bairns starving," replied George Arbuthnot.

"Maybe the Manager's right," said Amos, always the optimist. "Happen the machines'll help us win more coal and earn more money after all."

"Well, I say, give it a chance," said another miner. "If we find it's putting us out of work, then's the time to strike, not now."

There was a general murmur of agreement.

"Aye. True enough. I say we go back. Come on, lads."
They began to move off.

"At least have a vote!" shouted Luke. "We should put it
to the vote!"

The miners paused, glancing at each other.

"All right," said Big Alf. "We'll have a show of hands.
All those in favor of going back to work tomorrow?"

There was no need to count. Every miner, except for
Luke, raised his hand. Even little Amos, though he glanced
apologetically at Luke as he did so, voted to return.

"Those against?" said Big Alf.

Luke raised his hand. Dave, searching the crowd in vain
for more support, in desperation raised his own hand in
the air, and Tommy, glancing up at him, obediently raised
his hand, too. Only Luke saw this absurd gesture, and his
eye met Dave's for a moment. Dave was suddenly angry.
Luke had failed. He had done his best, no doubt, but he
had failed. His own father, thought Dave, would not have
failed. He turned and walked away, and Tommy slowly put
his hand down and followed him.

The miners were already moving away, but Luke stayed
where he was, his eyes on the two small figures as they
scrambled through the fence and disappeared. Then he
walked heavily after his companions towards the Manager's
office.

"Well?" said Mr. Sandman, coming to stand above them
on the balcony. "Have you decided?"

The men glanced at each other. Luke had been their
spokesman before. Big Alf stepped forward.

"We'll go back," he said.

His voice was surly, and Mr. Sandman gave no sign of
pleasure. He merely nodded, and returned to his office.
Sam Carter lingered behind.

"Well done, lads!" he cried, heartily. "Best report early
tomorrow, so as to get accustomed to the new ways."

But there was no answering look of cheerfulness from
the miners. Sam Carter was trying to pretend that they had
had a choice and had made the wise decision, but the
truth was that they had been beaten, and they knew it.

Mr. Sandman was at his desk when Sam went in, and
already planning the next day's work.

"We'll start in the forward heading," he said.

"Right, sir," Sam replied. He hesitated, and shifted from
foot to foot, and then cleared his throat. "It's—er—it's a

pity we can't find a home for the ponies. I was wondering if His Lordship wouldn't have a field somewhere, where they could . . ."

Mr. Sandman looked round, and Sam paused, before finishing, "I just thought it would have made it easier for the men to go back with a good heart."

"They would only have seen it as a sign of weakness," said Mr. Sandman, and bent again over his papers.

CHAPTER TWENTY

IT was almost like a normal day in Emsdale village next morning, with the miners coming out of their houses in their working clothes, carrying their safety lamps, their bait-boxes and dudleys. Almost, but not quite. There were no cheery greetings, and they tramped like a defeated army, avoiding each other's eyes. The women, too, as they stood at the doors to see them go, had a slightly shame-faced air, like hostages whose lives have been saved at the expense of a surrender, and who grudge the gift even as they accept it.

Mr. Sandman had his breakfast early, and was ready to leave by the time Alice came downstairs.

"Alice," said Mrs. Sandman, standing in the hall beside him while Mr. Sandman struggled into his overcoat, "Father is just leaving."

Alice paused for a moment, and then came down the final flight of stairs, and turned towards the dining-room.

"Aren't you going to kiss him good-bye?" said Mrs. Sandman.

Alice looked her father straight in the eye, and spoke in a clear, firm voice.

"I shall never kiss him again," she said, "as long as I live."

She walked into the dining-room, and Mr. Sandman took his hat from the hat-stand and walked out of the house.

The mechanized working of the colliery went ahead with surprising smoothness that morning. There was a certain amount of hostility between pitmen and engineers, and a good deal of profanity as the miners, those most conservative of all workers in the world, endeavored to get used to the new methods, changing the customs of centuries. But by noon, coal was being dug in the forward heading, and the main-and-tail hauler was in action, the full and empty tubs grinding to and fro.

Much of the efficiency of the changeover derived from the meticulous planning of Mr. Sandman. He had spent many hours on it during the closure of the pit, like a General preparing for a battle, and saw its outcome now with considerable satisfaction. He had given orders for the shipping of the ponies to Barnsley to go ahead, as originally arranged, and when they were led out, he was in his office, poring over schedules, costs and tonnages, and had, in fact, completely forgotten them.

Once more the ponies, anxious and resisting, were led out to the railway siding. There were few onlookers, the miners being either belowground, or busy about their work. Only Dave, grimly determined to see the last of them, had come with Tommy to watch the loading. The drivers were rougher than usual with the ponies—perhaps because they were afraid of showing any tender feelings, and perhaps, also, because the ponies, in a way, were responsible for the battle with the management which they had lost.

"Garn!" they yelled. "Get on there, will yuh? Yah!"

As Bluey was dragged towards the ramp which led up to the horse-truck, steam blew up from the engine, and he reared back and escaped from the hands of his driver, who swore and pursued him. Other men joined in the chase, and when he was caught, the driver jerked hard on the halter and struck him with his fist.

"Yer blamed stupid beast!" he shouted. "Get up there!"

Bluey put his ears back and rolled his eyes wildly, all his lively mischief subdued into the terror of a dumb beast driven uncomprehendingly to the slaughter, and Dave, watching, saw his nightmare come true.

Sam Carter, crossing the yard as Bert led Flash towards the truck, paused and threw an uneasy glance towards the Manager's office.

"Hurry up with loading them ponies!" he shouted. "Bert, take old Flash up, and then the others'll follow."

Bert led Flash, stumbling, towards the ramp. With that aching willingness to give always of his best, and more than he had to give, Flash strove to find his way blindly up the unfamiliar slope, floundered about, and went down on his knees. Dave felt the betrayed trust and bewilderment like a knife-wound in his own heart. He watched with set face and lips pressed close together, but Tommy slowly dissolved into tears, feeling for the first time that sharp-edged sorrow for the suffering of another creature which marks the first painful step to maturity.

But, while Bert was trying to jerk Flash's head up, and Flash tried to struggle to his feet, the whole yard and pit-head shook under the impact of a huge explosion. Dave saw a cloud of black dust rise hundreds of feet above the shaft. It fell upon the watchers in the yard, all frozen with their faces turned towards the pit-head in instantaneous comprehension of disaster.

Violet, scrubbing the kitchen floor, heard the explosion. She stayed there for a second, on her knees, and said one word, "Luke!" Then she got to her feet, and, without even waiting to take off the sacking apron which she wore, she snatched her shawl from its peg by the door and ran straight out of the house. She was joined by other women, old and young, some with babies in their arms, some clutching young children by the hand, but all, as they slipped and stumbled on the cobbles in their booted feet, had the same ghostlike look on their faces, as though their hearts and minds were already at the pit-head towards which they ran. When they were halfway there, the whistle began to blow with short, panicky blasts, shrieking in their heads like their own anguished dread.

Before the rumble of the explosion had died away, Mr. Sandman had risen from his desk, and was outside the door. He saw the black cloud above the shaft, and turned back into his office to snatch up helmet and overalls. As he ran down the iron staircase, he was joined by Sam Carter.

"Is the cage working?" he asked.

"I don't know."

They spoke curtly, but, strangely enough, it was the first time they had addressed each other without concealed hostility, but simply as two men who knew their job, and respected each other. A Deputy approached them, his face blackened.

"Cage is working."

"I'm going down," said Sandman, as he ran.

"I'll come with you," said Sam Carter.

By the time the first of the women reached the gates, they were already on their way down into the reeking pit.

As Violet, with the other women, came towards the pit-head, Tommy ran towards her. She put her arms round him, for a moment overcome by emotion, but then firmly controlled herself, and forced a smile and took his hand, turning towards the entrance to the cage with the same look of desperate inquiry as all the other women. Dave moved towards her more slowly. She had come because of her fears for Luke's safety, as she had once before come for his father. Dave did not resent it, as he would have earlier, but he felt awkward about it, as though he did not quite know what to say or do.

Alice heard the explosion while she was doing lessons in the schoolroom. She leaned forward, saw the black cloud of dust above the winding wheels and in a moment was on her feet and out of the room.

"Alice!" cried Miss Coutts. "What is that? Where are you going?"

But Alice had only one thought in her mind. Her father would not normally have been underground, but with the installation of the new machinery, he might have been.

"Father!" she said, and ran down the stairs and straight out of the front door.

The village street was deserted as Alice ran along it. Here and there, doors had been left open, and only Mrs. Binks stood in the doorway of her grocery shop, peering towards the pit-head. A widow from Huddersfield, she alone, in all the village, had no relative working in the mine.

When she reached the colliery gates, and saw all the women, Alice felt shy. She crept through the silent groups —so silent that her boots made a loud noise on the gritty ground—and looked in vain for her father. She knew that

he would not be in his office at such a time. She saw
Dave and Tommy, and realized that it must be their
mother who stood there with them, in her sacking apron,
with untidy hair and a black smudge of stove blacking on
her cheek. Alice was just wondering whether she could
catch Dave's eye, and get him to come over, so that she
could ask him if he knew where Mr. Sandman was, when
there was a sudden stir by the entrance to the cage.

"They're coming up!"

It was a stretcher which came out first, and Alice's heart
jumped, but then she saw Mr. Sandman, black-faced and
serious, stepping out of the cage, with Sam Carter just
behind him. The women surged forward, crying out for
news, but just at that moment there was another diversion.
A strange machine came through the colliery gates, with
cream-colored paint and silver trimmings. It crunched fas-
tidiously through the sludge and black puddles of the yard,
and crept to a halt. A chauffeur, trim and anonymous in a
maroon uniform, leaped out and opened the door, and
a tall figure emerged, wearing a cap and goggles, with a
dust-coat from neck to ankles. Lord Harrogate had arrived in his Rolls-Royce.

"Well?" said Lord Harrogate, with an unexpected note
of urgency.

"There's been an explosion, my Lord," said Mr. Sandman, "in a drift heading. We don't know yet what caused
it. No one was working there, but some men were injured
between there and the pit-bottom. We are getting them
out now."

He paused. In the dead silence, the crowd could hear
his words, as well as Lord Harrogate.

"Unfortunately, the explosion caused a fall, and . . ."
He stopped again.

"Well?" said Lord Harrogate.

"It would appear that a number of men are cut off in
the forward heading."

It was Violet who stepped forward from the other
wives and mothers.

"Who! Who are they?"

Mr. Sandman glanced inquiringly at Sam Carter.

"That's—Mrs. Armstrong, sir."

Mr. Sandman looked at Violet, and paused before speaking.

"I'm sorry, Mrs. Armstrong," he said. "I'm afraid your husband is one of them."

Dave looked at Violet, and saw her stricken face, and took hold of her other hand. She didn't look down, but she held his hand tight and he knew that she was glad of it.

Mr. Sandman spread a plan of the workings out on one of the huge empty crates which had held the machinery, and he, Lord Harrogate and Sam Carter bent over it together.

"Can't you get through to them?" asked Lord Harrogate.

"I don't know, my Lord. It isn't a very big fall, as far as we can judge, but it's knocked out the main ventilation shaft, and the afterdamp is very bad."

They all three bent over the map of the workings again. Because all their thoughts were bent upon rescuing the trapped men, Mr. Sandman and Carter found themselves addressing Lord Harrogate without that touch of obsequiousness which normally colored all their dealings with him, and he, too, under the shadow of death, seemed to take upon himself an honorable responsibility for those who worked in the mine, instead of merely looking upon it as an object for plunder.

"Isn't there any other way of getting through to them?" he asked.

"I'm afraid not, my Lord," Mr. Sandman replied. "It may be as much as a week before we can get the ventilation working well enough to allow us to get through from the main shaft, and there's no other way."

"Will they still be alive then?" inquired Lord Harrogate.

He had his answer in the glance which Sandman and Sam exchanged, before looking quickly at the women who crowded near. One of the Deputies broke the silence which followed.

"We'll get through to them somehow!" he shouted.

"Aye," said one of the miners who had escaped the blast and come up with the injured. "We'll dig through to them with our bare hands if need be. Come on, lads!"

There was a general shout and a move towards the shaft. Mr. Sandman's voice rose above the noise.

"I tell you, you'd be suffocated ten minutes after you left the shaft bottom!" he said.

They paused, and looked at him, checked by the authority in his voice. Mr. Sandman suddenly found all eyes upon him, waiting for him to tell them how the men could be saved, if not in that way—the miners, the women, even Lord Harrogate, waiting for him, the Manager, to tell them what to do. His mind struggled with the problem, as with a theorem to which there is only one answer, and that the wrong one. The men were trapped in the forward heading. The main roadway was choked with lethal afterdamp. There was no other way to reach them. And then he heard Dave's voice speaking from the edge of the crowd.

"We could get through from the old workings."

"The old workings?" repeated Mr. Sandman, with a quick frown.

"Aye," said Sam. "That's the way they brought the ponies out."

"Oh," said Mr. Sandman.

Because he did not want to think about Alice's involvement in it, he had paid as little attention as he could to what he had been told about the rescue of the ponies. He and Sam bent over the plans again, as Dave slipped through the crowd to stand beside them.

"You said you found the shaft on the far side of Napp's Hill?" said Sam.

"Yes. There."

Dave's dirty forefinger marked the place on the map.

"And they got the old winding-engine going, and all," said Bert.

Lord Harrogate's face brightened. He looked more like his old, irresponsible self.

"They did?" he said.

"Them and the Manager's Alice," said Bert.

Mr. Sandman was aware of Alice, standing in a gap in the crowd, listening intently, but he didn't look at her. He bent over the map again.

"If we could get down that shaft . . ." He looked up at Sam. "Could we get through from there?"

"We might," Sam replied, "but it's a regular maze in those old workings, and we don't know what state they'll be in after the explosion."

"Well," said Mr. Sandman, straightening up, "I'm prepared to try it."

"You'd be taking a terrible chance," said Sam. "We couldn't use anything but safety lamps, because of the danger of firedamp after the explosion, and there's not much light from them. In effect, you'd be traveling in the dark in a pit you don't know."

"I could show you the way!" cried Dave, eagerly.

"No, you couldn't," said Tommy, who had wriggled through the crowd to join him. "We got lost last time."

Dave glared at him.

"Anyway," said Sam, "we couldn't take the boy down."

"No, of course not," said Mr. Sandman.

"Flash knows the way," said Dave. "And he don't need any lights, neither."

There was a silence. Mr. Sandman looked from Sam to Dave and back again.

"Do you suppose the—the pony could find the way through?" He spoke with some reluctance.

"If it's Flash, he could," Sam replied. "When he's been there once, he can find his way again."

"Well," said Mr. Sandman, "I suppose it's worth a try." And then a terrible thought struck him.

"But—the ponies will have been shipped by now."

Even in the midst of his anxiety for the trapped men, he had time to feel a fool as he said it. To have made such an obstinate point of getting rid of the ponies at the earliest opportunity, and brooking no argument about it—and now, too late, to discover that he needed them!

"Nay," said Bert, "they've not gone yet. There's the engine driver."

Ostensibly to see if they could help, but in fact drawn by the irresistible fascination of disaster, the engine driver and his fireman had left their engine and their trucks and stood in their overalls in the yard.

"Right!" said Mr. Sandman, and his voice was strong and clear, as though he had just recovered from a long illness. "Come on, lads, let's see what we can do!"

The cavalcade which streamed out across the moors had something of the air of a circus as it travels from town to town. First went the horses and carts full of sledges, pickaxes and shovels, safety lamps and all the other paraphernalia of rescue. Then came the ponies, with Flash in the rear. Bert led him, and Dave held his mane to guide him. After the ponies came Lord Harrogate's Rolls-Royce, bouncing with as much dignity as it could manage over the rough moorland paths. And behind the Rolls followed a great throng of miners, wives and children, tramping along with heads held high, splendidly united in one hope and one purpose.

Alice had hung back a little, afraid of embarrassing her father, so she was in the tail-end of the procession when it passed the Sandman house. She saw her mother, standing at the garden gate, with Miss Coutts peering behind.

"Alice!" called Mrs. Sandman. "Where are you going?"

Alice paused, and then reluctantly made her way through the trailing women and children.

"To the old workings, Mother," she said. "There's been an explosion, and some men are trapped. Father is—" her voice trembled but she controlled it, "Father is going down, to try to rescue them."

Mrs. Sandman looked at her in silence for a moment, standing there in her white lace blouse and black skirt and jacket, and the neat hat with a veil without which she never stepped out of doors. Then she opened the gate, and came through it, and took Alice's hand.

"Come along, then," she said.

She clutched her skirts, and scrambled with Alice up the steep path which led up to the moors. Miss Coutts' voice came after them, shrill with horror.

"Mrs. Sandman! You are not going to—? Surely you are not going to—? With all those *miners' wives?*"

But Mrs. Sandman held Alice's hand in hers and walked firmly on across the moors behind the women in their clumsy boots and coarse skirts and shawls, as though she were one of them.

CHAPTER TWENTY-ONE

THE old engine thumped and puffed away, with Harry at the controls. A dozen strong hands stoked the fire which Alice, Dave and Tommy had had to struggle so hard to keep going. Pit props were stacked by the old shaft, in case it should be necessary to shore the roof up, and sledges were prepared for the transportation of injured men. It was dusk before the rescue could begin. A mine disaster draws like a grim magnet not only those most nearly concerned, but the curious for miles around. As Dave looked up from harnessing Flash, he saw on the rim of the hollow in which the old shaft stood, a circle of watchers, like vultures, outlined against the pale sky.

Mr. Sandman straightened up from the map of the old workings which he had been studying.

"Are we ready?" he said.

Sam Carter stepped forward. He was carrying a small cage with a canary in it.

"Ready, sir," he said.

"No, Sam," said Mr. Sandman, "you're not coming."

"I know the pit better than you do, sir."

"Yes, but I want you to stay here. If we—if we don't get through to the men, you'll have to find another way."

And because he had called him "Sam" and addressed him as one man to another, Sam Carter nodded. He gave him the birdcage.

"You'd best take this. It'll give you warning of foul air before owt else."

"Right," said Mr. Sandman. He turned towards the shaft and paused. "Is the pony there?"

Bert led Flash forward.

"Please, sir!" cried Dave, "let me go down with Flash!"

"No, it's out of the question," replied Mr. Sandman, brusquely.

And then his eyes fell on Dave's face. He saw him for the first time as a human being. He remembered how Luke had stood between Dave and Tommy and had said with that note of pride, "These are my two lads."

"I'm sorry, my boy," said Mr. Sandman, kindly. "I'm afraid I can't allow it."

He glanced towards Violet Armstrong, standing there in front of the other women, white but courageous.

"You stay and look after your mother," he said. "We'll get your father out if we can."

It was Ginger who stepped forward, carroty-haired and unprepossessing.

"I'll take Flash down," he said. "I'm his driver."

Ginger led Flash, stumbling, forward into the cage, and Mr. Sandman, in overalls and helmet, joined the other rescuers beside him. Sam Carter closed the bar over the opening.

"Good luck, sir," he said.

Sam rang the signal bell, and the cage slowly began to descend. Alice stood with Mrs. Sandman on the edge of the circle which silently ringed the old shaft. In the dim light, she could just see her father's face. "I will never kiss him again as long as I live," she had said. She had not spoken to him since, and now he was going down into darkness and danger. She took a step forward, but it was too late. The cage disappeared below the surface, and he was gone.

"Mr. Carter!" called Mrs. Sandman, as Sam turned away.

He stopped, and touched his helmet.

"The men who are trapped," said Mrs. Sandman, "do you think they are still alive?"

"That's the worst of it, Missus," replied Sam, glancing uneasily at Violet, "you never know until you get there."

Mrs. Sandman followed his gaze, and Violet managed to give her a slight, encouraging smile. It was unthinkable, of course, that Mrs. Sandman should smile back at a miner's wife, but she very nearly did. Then, very timidly, she moved closer to Violet, and Alice moved with her.

By the dim light of a safety lamp, the trapped miners crouched or lay in the small space left to them after the explosion and roof-fall.

"How's the leg feel, Amos?" asked Luke, kneeling beside him.

"Ugh! don't touch it!" Amos groaned.

"All right, lad. All right."

Luke sat back on his heels. With his great height, he had to bend his head down even so.

"Can you hear anything beyond the fall?" asked Amos.

"Not yet."

"If there's a build-up of afterdamp between here and the shaft, it could be days before they get through," said one of the miners, gloomily.

"Aye, Fred, cheer us up, why don't you?" said Big Alf, and Luke and Amos both grinned.

It was very cold in the irregular shaped cave which was their prison, and the injured men were shivering with shock as well. They were all conscious of their breath coming short, as the oxygen was inexorably drawn from the air. Indeed, "air" hardly seemed the right word for the thick, black substance which must be drawn into their lungs and expelled again. There was no vivifying freshness in it. It was only better than not breathing at all.

"I'm going up the other end," said Alf. "See if I can hear anything."

He began to crawl away in the direction of the blocked-off roadway, leaving the single glimmer of the lamp which barely held the darkness in check.

"Mind how you go, Alf!" Luke called. "That afterdamp can come on you before you know it, and if there's some firedamp mixed with it, then one spark from your boot would be enough to set it off."

"I'll creep like a little mouse," said Alf, and crunched and clattered noisily away.

Luke grinned again, and Amos did, too, but then grimaced with pain.

At the foot of the old shaft, Flash's trace gear had been harnessed to a sledge.

"I will go first," said Mr. Sandman. "If that plan of the old workings is accurate, I may be able to find the way."

Ginger knotted Flash's reins to the harness, and took hold of the bridle, to lead him. The little group of men took a firmer grasp of their lamps and sticks, and prepared to follow the Manager.

"Right?" said Mr. Sandman. "Come on, then. And watch your lamps for signs of firedamp."

In the dark cavern, Alf came crawling back, gasping for breath.

"By Goy, it's bad up there!" he said. "There's no one'll get to us that way, I'll tell you!"

He sat crouched with his head on his knees, trying to breathe again after the exertion.

"Could you hear anything at all?" asked one of the other miners.

"Not a sound. I reckon it'll be two or three days before the gas clears enough to let them through."

"Most like they think we're dead," said George Arbuthnot.

"It won't be long before they're right," said Fred.

"Eh, Fred, you *are* a tonic!" said Alf, and then they all laughed, and gasped and panted for breath, still trying to grin.

"Come and give me a hand, Alf," said Luke, after a moment. "I'm going to try and fix this pit-handle for Amos's leg."

Alf crawled over, and picked up the lamp, holding it up to give its dim light to Luke's ministrations.

"How much longer for the lamp?" asked Arbuthnot.

Luke and Alf glanced at each other.

"Not long," said Luke. "I want to get this done first."

Mr. Sandman, treading cautiously along the narrow roadway of the old workings, came to the place where the tunnel divided. He paused.

"Take my lamp," he said, and spread out the map, while his companions waited anxiously.

"Which way, sir?" asked the Deputy, as Mr. Sandman folded the map up again and put it in his pocket.

Mr. Sandman shook his head.

"It's not even marked," he said. He hesitated. "Bring the pony up to the front. See if he knows the way."

Ginger unknotted the reins, and let Flash walk forward.
"Go on, Flash!" he said.

"Go on, Flash!" the Deputy repeated. "Up to the coal-
face. Go on!"

Flash shook his head, and set off at a smart trot into
the darkness.

The stars had come out above the old pit-head. Flaring
torches illuminated the white, waiting faces, the ambulance vans, the scene of suspended activity. A quiet thump,
whir, thump from the old engine-house was the only sign
of motion. Dave, standing with Violet's hand in his, was
no longer aware of the scene about him. He saw, as clearly
as if he had been there, the sturdy little pony trotting confidently along in the darkness, master once more of his
own environment.

"Go on, Flash!" he said. His lips did not move, but he
knew it went straight from his mind to Flash's pricked
ears, "Go on, Flash!"

Luke tied the last knot on a makeshift splint consisting of
a pickaxe handle, scarves and handkerchiefs.

"Is that better?" he asked.

"Aye," said Amos. "Could walk twenty miles on it now."

"I daresay," said Luke, smiling, "but I wouldn't try it!"

The mere exertion of kneeling up and tying the knots
had left him breathless, and he sat back against the wall
of rock. Alf was bending over one of the other miners
whom they had dragged, injured, from the fall.

"How's Joe?" he asked.

"Poorly," said Alf. "He's poorly."

The lamp guttered and went out. They were left in the
darkness of a living tomb.

"Stop!" called Mr. Sandman.

Ginger hauled on Flash's reins.

"Whoa!" he said. "Whoa!"

Flash stopped instantly. The other rescuers came stooping after, their faces anxious.

"I'm going to test for firedamp," said Mr. Sandman.

He lowered the wick of his lamp, held the lamp high
and saw the telltale blue flame. He drew his breath in
sharply.

"It's loaded!" he said.

The Deputy, also looking at it, whistled. Mr. Sandman glanced at him, and at the other men for whose lives he was responsible.

"Well?" he said. "Shall we go on?"

Flash shook his head, and shifted impatiently a few steps forward. The miners glanced at each other, and back at Mr. Sandman.

"Aye, go on. Old Flash don't mean to stop, anyroad!"

"All right, Ginger," said Mr. Sandman.

He exchanged a smile with the Deputy. They both knew that he had had no intention of stopping, but he had done the right and courteous thing, and left the decision to the men. It was not something he could order them to do. Flash trod on, surefooted, along the dark, uneven passage, and they stumbled after him, but now they had ceased to be individuals, and had become a little band, united in a shared danger, deliberately undertaken.

Flash traveled more slowly, and several times paused before moving along a new passage. The Deputy glanced at Mr. Sandman, as they stooped along together, behind Ginger.

"Do you think he knows the way, sir?" he asked.

"I don't know," Mr. Sandman replied, with a touch of grimness.

But he knew that now they had no other recourse than to follow the pony, deeper and deeper into the black maze.

It was quite dark up by the old pit-head, except for the starlight, and the flaring torches, and the acetylene head-lamps of the Rolls-Royce, where Lord Harrogate sat in his white dust-coat, very upright, with a rug over his knees. The watchers grouped round the old shaft saw the chauffeur get out of the car and approach them, and Mrs. Sandman became aware that he was making his way towards *her*. He stopped in front of her, and touched his cap.

"Excuse me, Madam," he said. "His Lordship wondered if you would care to come and sit in the automobile."

Mrs. Sandman's face lit up. To be singled out for such an honor! To sit in aristocratic company in the stately motor car, exchanging polite conversation with Lord Harrogate—that was the height of her ambition! She actually took a step forward, and then she paused. Nearby, Violet was sorting out blankets with some of the other miners' wives, and though they did not look at her, she knew that

they had heard what the chauffeur had said. She stepped
back, and spoke to the man timidly, but with dignity.

"Would you thank His Lordship," she said, "but say that
I prefer to wait here."

"Very good, Madam," said the chauffeur.

He touched his cap again, and turned and walked back
towards the car. Mrs. Sandman, in her lace blouse and thin
jacket, was suddenly shivering with cold. It *would* have
been nice to sit in the warm. Probably she would never get
another chance to speak to Lord Harrogate. And then,
when he had been so kind as to ask her—had it been very
discourteous to refuse? Would he, perhaps, take offense?
She felt almost inclined to hurry after the chauffeur, calling
out, "Just a minute! I've changed my mind!" She felt a
touch on her arm, and looked down and saw Dave, holding
out a folded blanket.

"Me mother said, would you like to put this round
you?"

"Oh—thank you, dear," said Mrs. Sandman.

She took the blanket, and looked towards Violet and the
little group of women, and what she saw in their faces ban-
ished her last fragments of regret. She found Alice smiling
up at her, and smiled back, and together they unfolded the
blanket, and put it round them, cuddling up together in its
rough folds. And suddenly Mrs. Sandman, in spite of the
cold night wind which was springing up, felt quite warm,
after all.

In the forward heading, the darkness seemed to press suf-
focatingly down on the trapped men, as they crouched or
sat or lay, keeping close together for warmth.

"I can't breathe!" cried the boy, Dick, in a sudden panic.

"Yes, you can, lad," said Luke.

"But it's so dark!"

"What of it?" said Luke. "You don't need to see to
breathe. How would you manage at night, else?"

The boy was sitting beside him, propped against the
wall, and he felt him relax, and even try to laugh a little.

"Come on," he said, putting his arm round him. "You're
cold, that's all."

"Shall we try a hymn, lads?" said George Arbuthnot.

He was a fine tenor in the Chapel choir.

"Best save the air," said Big Alf.

"No point in saving it," said Fred. "There's no one coming. We know that."

"Oh, aye?" said Big Alf. "Say one thing more like that, and I'll use a bit of it up in coming across and clouting you. If you can't be cheerful, howd your gob!"

But, in fact, that made them all laugh a bit, although they paid for it in gasps and panting afterwards.

"At least we can say a psalm," said little George, and after a moment's thought, he began, *The Lord is my shepherd; I shall not want.*

The others joined in.

"He maketh me to lie down in green pastures: he leadeth me beside the still waters."

Far above them, they knew that heather was blowing purple over the moors, and rivulets of clear water ran down the rocks into the peaty soil.

"He restoreth my soul."

Did a man have a soul which lasted after death, and would they soon discover whether it was so or not?

"Yea, though I walk through the valley of the shadow of death, I will fear no evil: for thou art with me; thy rod and thy staff comfort me."

Dick's voice broke, and he stopped. He knew about God, but at that moment, he was afraid, and he wanted his mother. The other men carried on strongly to the end.

"Surely goodness and mercy will follow me all the days of my life: and I will dwell in the house of the Lord forever."

There was a silence after they had finished, broken only by gasps as they tried to draw their breath from the exhausted air about them. Then Alf spoke in a low tone.

"How long do you reckon, Luke?" he said

Luke was aware of Dick's face turning upwards on his chest to hear the answer.

"We know they're trying to reach us," he said. "We'll wait till they come."

Flash, trudging sturdily along, turned a corner and stopped short.

"Go on, Flash!" cried Ginger, slapping the reins on his back.

"What's the matter?" said Mr. Sandman, feeling his way forward.

He held the lamp up.

"He's brought us to a dead end," he exclaimed.

They looked at each other, disappointed.

"Well," said Mr. Sandman, "may as well turn back."

But it was such a disappointment that they all stood there for a moment.

"You're sure there's no way through, sir?" asked the Deputy.

"No," replied Mr. Sandman. "It's completely blocked off."

And he tapped the end of the passage with the stick.

"Just a minute," he said, and he tapped it again.

"What was that?" said Amos.

Luke roused himself from a sick doze.

"I didn't hear nothing."

"I did," said Alf. "It seemed to come from over there."

He crawled to the rock-face, found a piece of rock and knocked with it three times.

Mr. Sandman, about to turn away, stopped and turned back.

"Did you hear that?" he said.

He knocked twice, listened intently and heard two taps in reply.

"It's them!" he exclaimed.

"He's done it!" cried Ginger. "Old Flash! He's done it!"

And Flash tossed his head, as if to say, "Well, you idiot, what did you expect?"

The watchers at the pit-head saw a stir, and surged forward. A voice cried, "They've found them!" It was not a cheer which went up in reply, but a sort of moan of joy and hope and fear. Sam Carter hurried away from the pit-head.

"Doctor!" he called. "They need you down below!"

A rather stout man in a top hat and frock-coat was standing beside Lord Harrogate's car. He caught up his black bag and hurried towards Sam Carter, who came to meet him, and turned back with him. As they made their way through the crowd, the women called out.

"Who is it? Who's hurt? Are they alive?"

"I don't know yet," Sam called back. "I just know there's one man with a broken leg."

Violet didn't call out. She watched the doctor divest himself of frock-coat and hat, and Dave, glancing up at her, saw that she kept her eyes fixed with a desperate intensity on the cage as it descended. Although she stood with the other watchers, he knew that she was not aware of her skirt trailing in the mud, or of her shawl clutched against the cold wind. Her whole heart and mind were traveling down the old shaft and along the dark passages to discover whether her husband was alive or dead.

"Be careful!" said Mr. Sandman, sharply.

Under Mr. Sandman's direction, the little team of rescuers had tunneled through the fallen rock to reach the trapped men. With pit props they supported the broken roof which threatened more falls to crush them. And then with shovels and willing hands (sometimes bleeding from the jagged stone) they tore at the mass of fallen roof. Shovel, pass back, shore up and then on again a few more inches until they had made a tunnel through the fall, and, with the help of the other trapped men, were lifting the badly injured man through. Flash had been turned round, and was waiting with the sledge. The doctor helped to lay Joe on it, and wrapped him round with blankets.

"I can't do any more here," the doctor said. "Better get him to hospital as soon as possible."

"Right," said Mr. Sandman. "Go on, Ginger."

"Hey-up, Flash!" said Ginger, and Flash set off into the darkness.

The tense watchers at the pit-head started forward as they saw the cage arrive.

"Joe Snape!" Sam Carter called, and Mrs. Snape pushed her way through the crowd and ran to meet the stretcher as it was carried out.

"Joe!" she cried. "Joe!" and she ran beside him to the ambulance, with tears running down her cheeks.

"How is it?" asked Sam Carter of one of the rescuers who had come up with the injured man.

"Like a powder-keg," the man replied. "I only hope we can get them out before it all goes up."

Violet and Mrs. Sandman looked at each other quickly. Their eyes met, and they drew closer together.

"Quick as you can, Doctor," said Mr. Sandman, as the doctor climbed through the gap to attend to Amos.

"Right," said the doctor.

Stout as he was, he scrambled very nimbly down, making

room for the lugubrious Fred to clamber out. Mr. Sandman and the Deputy caught their breath as a spark flew from Fred's boot when he slipped on the loose stones, but Mr. Sandman spoke calmly and reassuringly.

"Can you walk?"

"Aye, I reckon so."

"Follow the lights, then. Parker, you go with him."

"What about you, sir?" said the Deputy. "Shan't we wait till—?"

"No," replied Mr. Sandman. "You get out while you can. I'll be along with the other men as soon as the doctor's finished. Tell Ginger to come straight back with the pony."

One by one the rescued men emerged at the pit-head, some walking, some carried, some on stretchers. As each name was called, their women broke through the crowd and ran to meet them. Young Dick rushed to the arms of his mother, and George Arbuthnot was hung about with wife and children until he could barely stagger. Each time, when they saw the stir before a name was called, Mrs. Sandman and Violet started forward, and then stood back, tensely waiting. But Alice only kept her eyes fixed on the place where she had last seen her father before he disappeared. She knew that, no matter who came up, he would be the last, and she remembered the words, "It's like a powder-keg."

Mr. Sandman and Luke waited with outward calm while the doctor worked on Amos's leg. He had decided not to replace the pickaxe handle with a proper splint, but only to bandage it more securely in place. He worked as meticulously as if he had been in the bedroom of one of his noble patients, repairing the damages caused by a hunting accident. It was admirable, of course, but as the doctor sat back on his heels to admire his handiwork, Luke, holding the lamp, glanced up at Mr. Sandman, and their eyes met in perfect accord.

"Ready, Doctor?" inquired Mr. Sandman, endeavoring to keep a sharp edge out of his voice.

"Yes, I think so," replied the doctor, calmly. "I can't do any more here."

"Right, then!" said Mr. Sandman. "Let's get him out!" and he found himself exchanging a grin with Luke, as they began to lift Amos through the gap.

Ginger had returned, with Flash, and they carefully laid

Amos on the sledge, and tucked the blankets round him. The doctor climbed through, and prepared to walk beside the sledge.

"You go with him," said Mr. Sandman to Luke.

"Are you coming?"

"In a minute," Mr. Sandman replied. "I'll just make sure there's no one else."

"Hey-up, Flash!" said Ginger, and the little procession set off, with the doctor and Luke walking beside the sledge.

Bill Parker, the Deputy, was waiting at the bottom of the shaft, and he helped Luke and the doctor to move Amos on to a stretcher, and lift it into the cage. Luke turned and saw Ginger unhitching Flash from the sledge.

"Go on, Ginger," he said, "up you go," and added, "You've done well, lad."

Ginger moved forward, looking surprised and gratified. Praise did not often come his way. He stepped into the cage in a glow of satisfaction. He knew that, as long as he lived, he would be known as the driver who had gone into the old workings and helped to get the trapped men out.

"Go on, Luke," said the Deputy. "I'll wait for the Manager."

Luke, stepping forward into the cage, did not see Flash moving quietly off into the darkness.

There was a cheer as the doctor stepped out of the cage, and turned to supervise the unloading of the stretcher.

"Amos Bradshaw!" called Sam Carter, and Amos's wife hurried to his side. Then, "Luke Armstrong!"

Like an arrow from a bow, Violet fled into his arms, and Tommy, running after her, was in a moment caught up on to Luke's shoulder. Dave would have liked to follow, but couldn't quite bring himself to do so. But he stood smiling, and his eyes met Luke's over his mother's head.

"Anyone else below, Luke?" asked Sam Carter.

"No, only Bill and the Manager, and they're on their way."

The cage had gone down again. There was a little stir and bustle as Amos was put into the horse ambulance, and then a silence fell, with all eyes once more on the top of the shaft. The cage rose above the surface, and came to rest, and Mr. Sandman stepped out. He was no longer the neat, dapper, well-polished Manager they had known. He was dirty and exhausted, in grimy overalls and a leather helmet. But as he came forward, a great cheer went up, and Mrs. Sandman, forgetting all dignity and decorum, ran to fling her arms round his neck and kiss him. Mr. Sandman heartily kissed her back, to redoubled cheers, and then he looked up and saw Alice standing timidly near. He held out his arms and she rushed into them. "I'm sorry," she cried, "I'm sorry!" and, as he held her close, the differences which had been between them vanished as though they had never been.

Lord Harrogate had descended from his car, and now approached Mr. Sandman.

"Well done, my dear Sandman!" he said. "Well done, indeed!"

"Thank you, my Lord," said Mr. Sandman, but although Lord Harrogate's commendation was welcome (not least because he had actually got his name right for once) the cheers of the miners and their wives rang still more pleasantly in his ears.

There cannot often have been a happier man in the world than Mr. Sandman as he turned away from the old shaft, with one arm round his wife and the other round his daughter. Harry shut down the old engine, and there was a general move, a general thought of hot soup and bed, and the idle watchers on the rim of the hollow began to withdraw, like playgoers when the curtain comes down and the theater lights go out. Only Dave still stood gazing at the old shaft.

"Where's Flash?" he said.

Mr. Sandman paused at once, and Luke, just moving off with Violet and Tommy, turned back.

"Hasn't he been brought up?" asked Mr. Sandman.

"He wasn't by the shaft," said the Deputy.

Ginger, proudly receiving the embraces of his mother and sisters, drew away from them, his face suddenly uneasy.

"I unhitched him from the sledge," he said. "I thought—" Ginger paused, and then finished, "I reckon he thought his shift was over, and he headed back for the stable."

They were all silent for a moment. They saw, as they had so often seen before, the sturdy little pony shaking himself until his harness rattled, tossing his bristly, parti-colored top-knot and setting off at a brisk trot into the dark passages where he alone could see.

Luke reached up and began to take Tommy down from his shoulder.

"I'll go and fetch him," he said.

"No, Luke, no!" cried Violet.

But Luke's eyes met hers as he put Tommy into her arms.

"I'm going," he said.

"Don't do it, Luke," said the Deputy. "If I know Flash, he'll've found his way through to the present workings. If you try to follow him——"

"Flash saved our lives!" said Luke. "I'm not going to leave him there!"

He went towards the shaft. Dave's eyes were fixed upon him with painful intensity.

"Luke!"

It was as though the word was forced from him. Luke turned to look at him, and suddenly Dave flung himself towards Luke and clasped him round the waist, and held him with all his strength.

"Don't go, Luke!" he said.

Luke was still hesitating, when from the direction of the old workings came a dull explosion. The earth shook under them, and dust rose above them. Luke bent over Dave, putting his own body protectively between him and the flying debris. As it subsided, Dave looked, anguished, up at Luke, and saw in his face all the concealed tenderness which he had never been able to show.

"Eh, lad!" said Luke. "Eh, lad!" and put his arms round him and held him close.

CHAPTER TWENTY-TWO

It was, after all, a dispirited procession which made its way up the path from the old pit-head. Even those who were not particularly fond of the pit ponies felt the loss of this one, and were oppressed by a sense of injustice that he should have saved the miners and perished himself. And then, there was the aftermath of all the exertion and excitement, the thought of the injured, and a slowly dawning anxiety about the effect of the explosion on the pit. Would Lord Harrogate be prepared to have the damage repaired or would the colliery remain closed forever? So, like an army which wins a victory but finds that the war is not won, they trudged slowly up the muddy path which led out on to the moors and the long walk home.

Lord Harrogate, standing by his Rolls, nodded to them all cheerfully as they went past, the men touching their caps, the women giving a little bob.

"Splendid!" he cried. "Well done, indeed! Good night! Good night!"

But he frowned a little, puzzled, as he saw Mr. and Mrs. Sandman and Alice bringing up the rear, and noticed that Alice was clinging to her mother with tears running down her cheeks.

"Sandman!" he called, and Mr. Sandman paused while his wife and daughter walked on. "A very good night's work, eh?" said Lord Harrogate.

"Yes, my Lord."

"Yes." He looked after Alice. "But—why do they all seem to be in such low spirits?"

"I think it is partly because of the death of the pony, my Lord," replied Mr. Sandman.

"The pony!" exclaimed Lord Harrogate, and began to laugh. "But, good heavens! What does a pit pony matter? The important thing is that all the men were saved!"

"Yes, my Lord," said Mr. Sandman. "That might make sense to—" he paused, "to outsiders. But the men have worked side by side in the pit with these ponies, and they mean a lot to them. They were distressed to think that they should be sent to the slaughter-house."

"Yes, yes, I daresay," said Lord Harrogate, "but surely . . ."

Suddenly Mr. Sandman had had enough of Lord Harrogate, standing there with his car and his chauffeur in his white dust-coat. What did he know of the way ordinary people felt?

"Good night, my Lord," he said brusquely, and walked on.

Lord Harrogate looked after him in astonishment.

Alice slept late next morning, but when she came down, she was glad to find her father still at the breakfast-table, and her mother pouring his second cup of coffee. Better still, Miss Coutts was not there.

"I'm afraid I have some bad news about your Governess," said Mr. Sandman, when Clara had brought Alice's porridge and retired.

"Oh, is she dead?" asked Alice, delighted.

"Alice!" exclaimed Mrs. Sandman, shocked.

Alice looked at her father. She thought that his lips twitched a little, but he shook his head at her severely.

"No, but I'm afraid she has given notice," he said.

"Oh," said Alice.

She took a spoonful of porridge, and looked up at him sideways.

"It appears that she has obtained a post with the family of a baronet outside Harrogate," said Mr. Sandman. "They are anxious that she should take up her position as soon as possible, and so I have given permission for her to leave at once. She is packing now."

"Oh," said Alice.

Try as she might, she could not help smiling. Mr. Sandman eyed her more severely than ever.

"You will have to have another governess," he said.

"Yes, Father," Alice replied, obediently.

"And this time," said Mr. Sandman, "we will try to find one who will endeavor to improve you, but not the whole family."

And then, suddenly, he was smiling broadly at Alice, and she was smiling back at him.

"Oh, really, Richard!" cried Mrs. Sandman, but, after all, she was smiling, too.

Clara came in with an envelope.

"This has just come by hand, sir," she said.

"Oh, Clara!" cried Mrs. Sandman. "Don't give it to the Master like that! You should put it on the silver tray."

"Oh," said Clara. "Yes, Mum. Shall I—?"

But Mr. Sandman had seen the bold black handwriting.

"Next time, Clara," he said, and took the envelope.

Lord Harrogate's note, as usual, was brief.

"Please come and see me this afternoon at 2 p.m."

Mr. Sandman read it through twice, and then rose, putting it in his pocket.

"I'd better get to the colliery," he said, "and see what the situation is."

"Oh, do be careful, dear!" said Mrs. Sandman.

"Don't worry," Mr. Sandman replied, "I shan't go below unless it's safe."

He went to the door and hesitated.

"I'm seeing Lord Harrogate at two o'clock," he said.

Alice looked at him quickly. Because she loved him, she didn't say what she wanted, but because he loved her, Mr. Sandman knew what she wanted to say.

"I'll try to talk to him about the ponies, Alice," he said.

"Oh, thank you, Father!"

"But I'm afraid it won't do any good. He—doesn't understand."

Alice nodded and tried to smile at him.

"I'm very sorry, dear," he said. "I'd take care of them myself if I could. But there isn't room in our paddock for them. There's only just enough room for Baron. And even if there *were* room for the ponies—which there isn't—I couldn't afford to feed them."

"No, Father," said Alice. "It's all right. I understand. Really."

Driving to Harrogate House that afternoon, Mr. Sandman tried to prepare himself for the coming encounter. It wasn't easy, of course, to prepare yourself for a meeting with Lord Harrogate, because you never quite knew what he would be doing. (Patent letter-opener? Mechanical shoe-polisher?) But Mr. Sandman, when he came within sight of the house, reined in the black horse, Baron, and sat marshaling his thoughts. The most important thing was to ensure that the colliery would be reopened. Lord Harrogate would be pleased to hear, surely, that the new machinery appeared to be mainly undamaged. The cause of the accident was not quite certain—perhaps it never would be entirely established—but it seemed likely from what the injured engineer had said that the explosion had been caused by an electrical fault, causing a spark which had ignited a pocket of firedamp. As soon as they could get the ventilation working again, they would be able to clear the fall—which by all accounts was not a large one—and then work at the coal-face could start in a compara-tively short time. Surely Lord Harrogate would agree that it would be far better to work the colliery and begin to pay off the cost of the machinery than to close the pit and waste the money already spent?

Yes, thought Mr. Sandman, that was the argument which he must put forward. He clicked his teeth and the horse moved forward. And then, he thought, when he had convinced the owner of *that*, then perhaps he could get round to speaking about the ponies.

Mr. Sandman thought that the butler looked at him pityingly as he took his hat. Servants, he thought, always knew first what their masters were doing. Did Barker know that Lord Harrogate had already decided to cut his losses and close the pit?

"His Lordship is in the garden, sir," said the butler.

Mr. Sandman walked across the marble hall like an officer captured in enemy territory. But at least, he thought, he would not go down without a fight. And if he could not save himself, he would try to save his men.

The butler led the way through the conservatory and down the stone steps. Lord Harrogate was peering at a rose-bush. Mr. Sandman's heart sank as he saw at Lord Harrogate's feet a large bucket, and in his hand a sort of bulbous air-gun. Presumably he was engaged in spraying the greenfly. I don't care, thought Mr. Sandman. I shall take it away from him. I shall *make* him listen.

"Mr. Sandman, m'Lord," pronounced the butler, with regret.

Lord Harrogate turned. Mr. Sandman took a deep breath.

"Ah, Sanderton," said Lord Harrogate. "Going to get the colliery working again soon, are you?"

"Er—yes, my Lord," said Sandman.

"Good," said Lord Harrogate. "Good."

He plunged the sprayer into the bucket.

"Now," he said, "what are we going to do about those ponies?"

CHAPTER TWENTY-THREE

WITH a triumphant oom-pa-pah! and a flourish of red, blue and gold satin banners, the Emsdale Colliery Brass Band marched down the street. Behind it walked the miners and their wives and children. The men wore their best dark suits, with cloth caps, and had white scarves knotted about their throats. The women wore spotless white aprons over their dresses, and artificial flowers and cherries in their straw hats. The girls' pinafores were starched so crisply that an ounce more would have made them crack, and the boys, starting out as neat and trim as their Sunday best of cut-down suits and bulky gray home-knitted stockings would allow, were busily engaged in making their Sunday best dirty in the shortest possible time, by walking through puddles, pulling twigs from the hedges and, if all else failed, tripping each other up and rolling on each other in the ditches. Oom-pa-pah! went the brass band as they turned the corner into the lane and went marching along beside the high wall and through the great gates, and set out on the private road which led through the parkland towards Harrogate House.

Mr. and Mrs. Sandman had driven over with Alice a little earlier, and were waiting by the terrace. They looked rather nervous, especially Mrs. Sandman, who had yet to meet Lord Harrogate. Alice was in her best white frilly dress, with a pink sash and a pink hair-ribbon. She wished that she could have marched up from the village with Dave and Tommy. She was uneasily conscious of having an important duty to perform, and was afraid that she might not do it properly.

The terrace was decorated with red, white and blue bunting, and before it, on the lawn, were set out long trestle tables and benches. Parlormaids and footmen were hard at work about the tables, which were covered with white cloths, and festive with jellies, cakes and glass bowls of strawberry jam. There were large, flowered plates of bread and butter, cut in triangles a quarter of an inch thick to satisfy the appetites of the boys, and spread thick with butter to please everyone. Mrs. Ramsbottom's scones, too, were heavily buttered and piled high, with tea-towels laid over them and the bread and butter to keep them moist until the guests were ready to sit down.

Distantly on the sunny air came the sound of the brass band approaching across the park—a slightly ragged sound, since they were running short of breath. There was a final flurry round the tea-tables, and Albert, the boot-boy, got his ears boxed for filching a scone when he thought no one was looking. He did not, however, surrender the scone, which he had crammed into his mouth whole. The butler and Mrs. Ramsbottom placed themselves in the midst of the other servants, ranged in strict order of precedence behind the tea-tables, as Lord Harrogate came out on the terrace.

"Welcome!" he cried, as the procession formed itself into an orderly and expectant throng below the terrace. "Very glad to see you all. Very glad indeed. As you see, Mrs. Ramsbottom has got a splendid tea for you, and the cakes should be particularly good, because she has baked them in the new electric oven which I sent for specially from London."

This was too much for Mrs. Ramsbottom.

"If His Lordship thinks I'd bake my cakes in that nasty

machine of his," she said, in a penetrating aside, "he doesn't know as much as he thinks he does!"

Lord Harrogate did not seem to hear. "Before we start on this excellent tea and—er—cakes," he said, with a touch of haste, "we have a ceremony to perform. Come along, everyone! Come along!"

Cheerfully waving his panama hat, he descended the terrace steps, and led the way round the side of the house.

A sunny pasture, rich with green grass, buttercups and daisies, ran down to the river. The five-barred gate stood open, and across the gateway was stretched a white ribbon. The miners raised a cheer when they saw the pit-ponies standing in a restless group beside the field, with Bert, Dave and Tommy in charge of them. Small heads tossed impatiently and small hooves shifted in the grass as Lord Harrogate mounted a slightly rickety rostrum, decorated with red, white and blue ribbons. Alice came to stand with her mother and father in the front row. She didn't feel nervous any more. She was too excited.

Lord Harrogate cleared his throat, and mothers hastily shushed the assorted small boys who ran around, hit each other, attempted somersaults or otherwise did their best to mar the solemnity of the occasion.

"Well now," said His Lordship, with a happy smile, "I am very glad to see you all here today. It is excellent news that Emsdale Colliery is once more in full working order. The new machinery is properly installed, and will soon provide plenty of work for everyone."

There was a hearty cheer.

"And I hope," Lord Harrogate added, "that before long it will also ensure a good profit from the colliery for *me*."

There was a second cheer, almost as loud as the first. A more suspicious peer than Lord Harrogate might have wondered whether there was not more than a touch of irony this time, and might even have noticed the miners glancing at each other and grinning. But Lord Harrogate was innocently delighted.

"How kind of you, my good fellows," he said. "Thank you. Thank you."

The miners grinned more than ever, and their wives frowned at them reprovingly, and then looked down, hiding smiles.

Lord Harrogate continued with renewed enthusiasm.

"We are very grateful," he said, "that no lives were

lost in the recent disaster, and I am sure we are all agreed that the new Manager showed great courage and resource during the rescue operations."

There was no mistaking the genuineness and spontaneity of the cheers and applause which greeted this remark. Mr. Sandman was taken completely by surprise. He had never dreamed of such a thing. He looked down in embarrassment, and then, as the cheers were prolonged, he glanced round at the miners. He no longer saw them as a crowd of anonymous men who would only work if he made them work. He saw Tom and Alf and George, with whom he had crawled through dark, unknown passages, sharing their fear as they had shared his. He was startled to observe that Luke was applauding more loudly than anyone.

"Nay," thought Mr. Sandman to himself, in pure Yorkshire, "but it was a good fight, and fairly fought on both sides."

And they had ended, he thought, by fighting together against death—which, come to think of it, was how all battles must end.

The cheers died down, and his eyes met Sam Carter's.

"Well done, sir," said Sam.

"Thank you, Sam," said Mr. Sandman.

And they smiled at each other.

Lord Harrogate was speaking again.

"Now then," he said, "we mustn't forget that we are all here for a very special purpose. Barker!"

The butler moved towards Alice, carrying a silver tray on which reposed a large pair of scissors. Alice seized them and looked up at Lord Harrogate.

"Now?" she cried, eagerly.

"Not just yet!" replied Lord Harrogate, quickly.

He very much enjoyed making speeches, and felt that this one was going well. He had no intention of cutting it short.

"We are all aware," he said, "of the part played in the rescue by one of our faithful friends, the pit ponies. Unfortunately, Flash is no longer with us, but in his honor, I have much pleasure in donating this field, in which his companions will be able to live for the rest of their lives in comfort and freedom."

Lord Harrogate beamed upon his audience. He was only too pleased that other people should be happy, as long as it didn't interfere in any way with his own pleasure and comfort.

"I now call upon Miss Alice Sandman," he said, "to cut the ribbon!"

There was a silence as Alice walked to the ribbon. For a moment, they all thought of the bad things—of the strike, of the Arbuthnot children crying for hunger and of the miners trudging back, beaten, to the colliery, of the terror of the explosion and of the injuries from which the men were only just recovering.

Alice looked at her father. She was remembering the awful weeks when it seemed as though they would never love each other again. He smiled at her encouragingly, but she only just smiled back. Perhaps it was because even her very happiness at that moment reminded her that happiness was a fragile thing, and always incomplete. There was, after all, no parti-colored top-knot bobbing among the heads by the entrance to the field. Then she looked at Dave and Tommy, and she forgot everything else.

"We did it!" she thought. "We tried to save the ponies, and we did it!"

She held the scissors poised above the ribbon, and looked inquiringly at Dave. She felt that this was something which they must do together. Dave nodded, and Tommy grinned his gap-toothed grin and Alice cut the ribbon.

In a joyous surge of energy, the ponies rushed out into the field. They kicked their little hooves in the air, and tossed their short manes, and Dave and Alice and Tommy ran beside them.

"Come, Bluey! Soldier, Star! Come, True!"

"Sandy, True, Jester!"

"Come, Bluey! Come, Lion!"

And soon all the other children had joined them, dancing and laughing with the ponies in the sunshine.

"Tea, everyone!" cried Lord Harrogate. "Tea!"

Wooden chairs had been placed in a circle for the band at the end of the terrace, and, refreshed by the pause, they began to play with new enthusiasm as everyone sat down. Lord Harrogate walked up and down the long tables, watching benevolently as cups of tea were carried from the big silver urns, and plates of bread and butter were passed to and fro.

"Well done, everyone!" he cried. "Eat up! Splendid! Splendid!"

Somewhat to their dismay, he patted several children on the head, and passed some strawberry jam to several miners who would have preferred potted meat, and then, happily assured that they were all being cared for, he mounted the steps to the terrace.

Here a tea-table had been set out, with a lace cloth and silver teapot, for a more select gathering, consisting of the Rector, the Doctor and his wife and the Sandmans.

"Ah, Sandiman!" he exclaimed. "That all went very well, hey?"

"Very well, indeed, my Lord."

"I thought the men seemed to appreciate my speech."

"Yes, indeed, my Lord," said Mr. Sandman.

He salved his conscience with the reflection that the miners had, indeed, enjoyed the speech in their own way. Lord Harrogate's eyes traveled on to Mrs. Sandman.

"May I introduce my wife, my Lord," said Mr. Sandman, and added hopefully, "er—Mrs. Sandman."

Lord Harrogate shook Mrs. Sandman enthusiastically by the hand.

"How d'you do? How d'you do?" he said. "Awf'ly pleased, Mrs. Sanderton. And this," he added, turning to Alice, "this is the young lady who got the winding engine working, eh?"

"Well, I helped," said Alice. "I knew how to put it together, but I couldn't make it work by myself."

"Ah," said Lord Harrogate, with all the sympathy of fellow-feeling. "Quite so." He turned back to Mrs. Sandman. "I daresay you're interested in engines as well, Mrs. Sandstone?" he inquired, hopefully.

"Oh yes, my Lord," Mrs. Sandman cried, eagerly.

If Lord Harrogate had inquired as to her interest in the breeding habits of the lesser molluscs, she would have acquiesced no less readily.

"Good, good," said Lord Harrogate. "I have a little machine which I'm sure you'd like to see."

"Oh yes, my Lord," Mrs. Sandman agreed. "Certainly I would."

"Barker," said Lord Harrogate casually, as the butler

approached to serve the tea, "bring the egg-timer here, will you?"

"Very good, my Lord," said the butler, in a voice of gloomy foreboding.

"I know you'll be interested to see this," said Lord Harrogate, to Mrs. Sandman. "The whole thing works from an electrical accumulator. Turns out a four-minute egg, perfectly cooked, every time. Just the sort of thing you might like to have at home."

"Oh yes, my Lord!" cried Mrs. Sandman.

She did not know, as the butler did, that either the egg lurked uncooked in obstinately cold water, or else it shot through the aperture like a bullet from a gun, and splattered half-boiled all over the table. Lord Harrogate was delighted by her enthusiasm.

"Splendid!" he cried. "Now then, you sit here, by me."

Mrs. Sandman sat down in the place of honor, on Lord Harrogate's right hand, and there was one tiny flaw in her happiness. It was that Miss Coutts was not there to see.

The Armstrong family had found places at the end of one of the long tables. Like everyone else, they were laughing when they sat down, enjoying the sunshine and the band, and the sight of the generously loaded tables, and the sensation of being waited on by footmen and parlormaids. But gradually Dave found his smile fading, and the bread and butter and potted meat which he had taken with such enthusiasm seemed to turn heavy and unwelcome in his mouth. He glanced at Luke, who was chuckling with Amos over Lord Harrogate's speech, and at Violet, who was busy wiping an excess of strawberry jam from Tommy's face, and then he looked down the long table of chattering, smiling, eating people. They didn't care. None of them cared. Flash had died, and nobody cared, just as nobody had really cared when his father died. Dave suddenly felt very lonely, and because it was much worse to sit there among all those cheerful people and feel as he did, he slipped quietly off the end of the bench and walked away, round the corner of the house.

Old Lion had begun to graze, but most of the ponies were still frisking about, kicking up their heels at each other and galloping about with that heavy-quartered, rocking-horse gait of theirs. Dave climbed on to the lowest bar of the gate and leaned over the top, watching them. He could hear from a distance all the noise of happy voices and the clatter of crockery, and the sound of the band playing slightly out of tune, and he felt lonelier than ever.

A voice behind him said, "Dave?"

He knew who it was, but he didn't look round. He didn't know if he was glad or sorry when Luke came and leaned on the gate beside him. But after a while, Luke said, "He was the best of them all, was Flash," and then Dave did feel a minute lessening of the heavy weight on his heart. There was, after all, one person who felt as he did. There was one other person who cared. And then Luke added, "It seems it's always the best that go."

Dave kept very still. It was as though he was waiting for something very important to happen, and he could not move until it did.

"Your father," said Luke, "was the best friend I ever had. I reckon I'll miss him till my dying day."

Dave turned, then, and Luke looked him straight in the eyes.

"And you will, too," Luke said.

Dave could not answer him. He was afraid that he might do something stupid like bursting into tears. They both looked again at the ponies, where Jester had ill-advisedly started nibbling at the same tuft of grass as Bluey. There was an alarming but comparatively harmless thud of Bluey's hooves on Jester's thick coat.

"Eh, that Jester!" said Luke. "He'd best keep clear of Bluey if he wants to keep a set of whole ribs!"

Dave nodded and smiled. The silence which followed was very companionable, as they watched Soldier rolling luxuriously in the grass, and Star and True galloping down by the river, whickering and nipping each other. The daisies and buttercups shone like stars about them.

"I wish it could have been Flash," said Luke, "out there in the sunshine."

"No," said Dave.

It was as though the anger and resentment which Dave had felt against Luke had prevented him from seeing the truth, and now he broke through the obstruction and left it behind him, like breaking through the barriers between the old workings and the new.

"No," he said. "It's better as it is. When he was above ground, Flash *knew* that he was blind."

Luke nodded slowly. They looked at each other, and both felt the beginning of a friendship which was to last for the rest of their lives.

Violet, coming round the corner of the big house, saw Dave and Luke standing there together. She paused, and a look of radiant happiness came into her face.

"Well," she called, "are you going to stand there all day, looking at ponies, or are you going to come and have some tea?"

Dave and Luke grinned at each other, and turned and began to walk towards Violet and the busy tea-tables and the oompa-ing band. The ponies ran free in the sunshine, and, beyond them, the winding wheels of Emsdale Colliery were etched black against the summer sky.

Mr. Sammann looked at Violet, and paused before speaking.